"Kielland astonishes through an impressive ability to convey how choices compound and become unbearable to one's inner life—abetted by Damion Searls' painstakingly careful translation."
—Alexander Pyles, *On the Seawall*

"A short, sharp shock of a book . . . [*My Men* is] a singular novel of unusual power from a fearless and remarkable writer."
—Carys Davies, *The Guardian*

"Kielland's lyrical, abstract, and visceral prose, capably translated by Damion Searls, has won acclaim in her native Norway and is a beguiling match to her terrifying subject matter."
—Molly Odintz, *Literary Hub*

"[*My Men*] offers both a dark twist on the immigrant novel and a lyrical retelling of a gripping true-crime case. . . . Kielland rejects the trauma-revenge plot for something more powerful and haunting. . . . The novel's prose is characterized by a highly saturated, ripe sensuality that remains palpable and powerful in the translation by Damion Searls."
—Anushka Joshi, *The Rumpus*

"This novel turns the tropes of true crime on its head."
—Michael Barron, *The Rumpus*

"*My Men* is a great read at first instance, but is also the kind of book that, I feel, would reward a second pass in that Jordan Peele kind of way. I'm definitely going back." —Bram Presser, *A Book for Ants*

"*My Men* paints an extraordinary portrait of the inner turmoil and ecstasy of the woman widely regarded to be America's first female serial killer, Belle Gunness." —Catherin⁓ ⁓ *Marie Claire* (UK)

T0182734

"Kielland's pithy tale lingers long after the reader is finished. In addition to historical fiction readers, aficionados of both crime fiction and Scandinavian literature will welcome this award-winning voice to the table." —Karen Clements, *Booklist*

"Thoroughly hypnotic in both language and plot, Victoria Kielland has created an intimate and raw portrait of the ruthless pursuit of the 'American Dream.'" —Michael Welch, *Chicago Review of Books*

"Entirely chilling." —Sara Batkie, *Chicago Review of Books*

"[A] provocative English-language debut . . . [Belle Gunness's] spiritual yearning and profane desires are captured in dynamic and subversive prose. . . . It's an impressive feat of historical imagination." —*Publishers Weekly*

"Victoria Kielland's *My Men* doesn't take a sensationalistic approach; instead, this novel provides an impressionistic version of Gunness's story, illustrating her struggle for control over her own life and the increasingly lethal forms that control ends up taking." —Tobias Carroll, *Words Without Borders*

"This is a poetic, heartbreaking novel about a woman, Belle, who has endured a brutal act of misogynistic violence, and emigrates from Norway to America to start a new life. . . . I'll be thinking about Belle for a long time." —Tracey Thompson, *California Reading*

"[*My Men*] is the rare quiet literary thriller that haunts with its lyricism and exquisitely wrought characters." —David Gutowski, *Largehearted Boy*

PRAISE FOR *MY MEN*

"*My Men*, superbly translated by Damion Searls, is a portrait of a woman trying, and failing, to escape her punishing trajectory. Bit by bit, day by day, we see, and come to understand, what has made Belle Gunness a killer."

—Sarah Weinman, *The New York Times Book Review*

"*My Men* is a stylistic tour de force. . . . It reads like an expressionist prose-poem penned by a stark-minded zealot. . . . Kielland is clearly a gifted writer, and *My Men* is an impressively realized creation."

—Tom Nolan, *The Wall Street Journal*

"This fascinating, off-kilter novel about a female serial killer is an unexpectedly thrilling read."
—Karl Ove Knausgård, author of *My Struggle* and *The Morning Star*

"Kielland's dense, lyrical novel offers both insight and opacity. . . . Despite the subject matter, this novel is not your typical thriller. The language, in Searls' translation, is dense, poetic, and deeply figurative." —*Kirkus Reviews*

MY MEN

VICTORIA KIELLAND

Translated from the Norwegian by
Damion Searls

ASTRA HOUSE ∧ NEW YORK

Astra House
A Division of Astra Publishing House
astrahouse.com
Printed in the United States of America

Library of Congress Cataloging-in-Publication Data
Names: Kielland, Victoria, author. | Searls, Damion, translator.
Title: My men / Victoria Kielland ; translated from the Norwegian by Damion Searls.
Other titles: Mine menn. English
Description: [New York] : Astra House, [2023] | Summary: "Based on the true story of Norwegian maid turned Midwestern farmwife Belle Gunness, the first female serial killer in American history. My Men is a fictional account of one broken woman's descent into inescapable madness."-- Provided by publisher.
Identifiers: LCCN 2023007137 | ISBN 9781662601927 (hardback) | ISBN 9781662601934 (ebook)
Subjects: LCSH: Gunness, Belle, 1859-1908--Fiction. | LCGFT: Biographical fiction. | Novels.
Classification: LCC PT8952.21.I38 M5613 2023 | DDC 839.823/8--dc23/ eng/20230227
LC record available at https://lccn.loc.gov/2023007137
ISBN: 9781662602993 (pb)

This translation has been published with the financial support of NORLA.

NORLA
NORWEGIAN LITERATURE ABROAD

First paperback edition, 2024
1 3 5 7 9 8 6 4 2
Designed and typeset by Tetragon, London.

Love tends to go ever further and further,
but there is a limit.
When the limit is passed
love turns to hate.
To avoid this change
love has to become different.

SIMONE WEIL
"Love," in *Gravity and Grace*

I lived to lift you up
But who would lift me up?
When you were up among the clouds
And I was lying here on the ground

MOLLY SANDÉN,
"Without You"

To my dearest love, E.

BABY

SKANDINAVEN NORWEGIAN-LANGUAGE NEWSPAPER, CHICAGO, 1904–1908

Offer of Matrimony – Farmer, 26, in N. Dakota, Few Aquaintances, seeks to correspond with Scandinavian Girl or Widow. Financial situation not Important. Serious Replies only. Include photo.

Offer of Matrimony – Bachelor, 30, good-looking, Affluent, lives in a City, wishes to correspond with a Girl under 30 who knows how to appreciate the value of a Beautiful Home. Send photo in first Letter.

Offer of Matrimony – Widower, 45, looking to meet a Girl or childless Widow of Norwegian background, between 25 and 40. Strong references available and required. I can provide a good home free of cares since I am in good Financial circumstances. Address available from this Paper.

CITY OF ANGELS, CALIFORNIA, 1915

T ONGUES OF FLAME flickered in the fireplace, hot and silent. Belle needed a window to rest her cheek on, to cool her skin, glowing red, fresh as dew, calm and hot. These little mustache hairs, she ran her fingers over her lips and heard her murmuring lungs. She lit a cigarette and looked out at the city. The enormous oak tree in the evening sun reached its long, gnarled roots along the wall and into the ground; the roots coiled around the fence, crept out under the grass. Clotheslines ran between the branches, sheets and panties flapping gently in the wind.

There are things I can't ever admit, she whispered, *things that are too big, too much*, she could hardly breathe, *that could destroy me*. The words grabbed her by the throat, Belle didn't know when it was all going to snap, but she knew it would. A bullet, an inverted lung, a postscript to a thousand wars, tears ran down her face, *there're too many of you*. She felt her stomach turn, in the darkness, one muscle after the other.

The evening sun was low in the sky, her upper lip had chapped and split right down the middle, she took a deep drag of the cigarette; little words, almost a little scream, filled her mouth between the smoke and the teeth, tickling her gums, forcing their way out between her slack lips, *no one who loves with their whole self can survive it.* The waves of the Pacific rolled restlessly up onto the shore, the dark shimmer shone up toward her, and her voice filled the whole room, a truth so huge that it stood in everything else's way. The words reached toward the window, there was something about the little wrinkles around her eyes, her skin's little traces of everything that had happened, of time's furrowed face, of all the problems lurking in her lungs, Belle felt it with perfect clarity, the shimmer, the salt water almost blinding her, *there're too many of you.*

RØDDE FARM, 1876

B RYNHILD'S HEAD was wrapped in darkness. It was being pushed down into the pillow, face-first. All the colors piled up, her heart beat hard, a pulsing knot of muscle in the middle of the sunset, throbbing red, glowing hot. Everything she was going to see and feel, face-first. Everything she was going to experience. Brynhild slipped back and forth between sweat and dream, floated in darkness as spit dribbled down from her open mouth. The bed creaked, she tensed every muscle in her body and raised her head to the window, the tiniest little movement, it took all she had. Brynhild saw the starry sky prickling, she filled her lungs with air before sinking back down onto the mattress. The dim light of the paraffin candles reached into the room, covered the walls with flickering shadows. Brynhild saw the outlines of her own body against the wall, intermittent, layered, she felt him on top of her, breath on the back of her neck, tongue drawing new lines there.

Brynhild had taken her clothes off so fast, seventeen years old, so gentle and good, so ready for the world, she'd been ready since the second she saw him, when she straddled his lap, *I know you want me.* Desires erupted from nowhere, glowing, sudden, the candlelight fluttered in the window frame and there, then, they hovered in the flame, afire and flowing. This was love. No one could tell her otherwise. God was here, so close, and an oily black light filled the bedroom. A thick sauce of something manmade tossed and turned on the mattress. He was so taut and bright, his worthless beautiful body, there was no doubt about it, she loved this man. She felt it in her bones, the craving in her belly, the colors diluting themselves on their own, one sensation slipping unresistant into the other no beginning no end all there in one big pool of sweaty muscles and blurry passings back and forth. Brynhild had undone her braid and her hair streamed down over her shoulders and he'd looked at her sitting on top of him with her starry blue eyes in that milk-white face, those pinkish cheeks, pale freckles, brown hair everywhere, she had bloomed and opened like a dark flower. The anticipation in two strange eyes, that color palette, all that softness and innocence laid so bare. And the sky really had fallen down to earth that night, pressing down on the house, it had pricked against Brynhild's skin and she'd felt the stars on her eyes, they'd stung and burned, there was so much hope, endless hope, in a dark blue sky.

7

A new canvas had been stretched onto the frame, the black dirty love-sweat had scattered its seed, the rich farmer's son from Selbu had walked straight into the attic room, straight between her two half-open lips, straight into her open mouth. He'd taken her into his arms and she'd leaned into him and he'd seduced her with both hands. A touch that made her melt, rocking hips, she took, he gave, convulsing, bit by bit, she lay there for days, shoved into the darkness. That's how it happened, she'd been raised up high in the name of love and now she was vibrating, she couldn't stop trembling. A gentle breeze drifted through the curtains, *I can die now*, but she didn't die, she was breathing, she panted like a wet little dog, glowing with the morning sun right in her face.

Young Brynhild quivered against the sheets, all alone, she was so far from home, from mom and dad and the sheep up on the hill, she could feel it down in her bones, the fumbling, all the uncertainty, everything her eyes had seen the night before. It was a fairy tale, red like the dawn, sheets soaked and stained in a hundred different shapes. Brynhild traced the outlines of the stains with her finger, the spots clearly drawn in the sharp morning light, and she wiped her hand on her thigh. Everything she'd seen the night before, everything that had no words for it, the intense eyes resting on her. Broiling sunbeams pierced the window, thoughts sat in the middle of her head, her ears were listening for the least little movement, the thread of life was stretched tight.

Firstborn came back, a huge mass of skin and a wide white smile, so loving and strict, so strong, so addicted to his own desire. This man with pale hair and the smell of dirt and soft leather, boots that squeaked and scratched against the bedframe. Brynhild's body felt the benediction, the weight in the darkness, the golden shimmer in the heart, it went from soft to hard so fast she didn't realize what had happened. The dark passion when there was no more daylight, hands that could so suddenly ball into fists. Everything that changed as soon as she wasn't looking. Little negotiations every single time. All the colors up against her eyes. The forever-warm body. Her head pushed down into the pillow every night. Mouth open till it poured and she had to swallow. The jolting ran through her like night-black shivers through the room.

Brynhild lay sunk into the mattress. She lay there with the farmholder class on top of her, a defenseless condition, totally naked, totally unprotected with her whole melting little tip sticking out into the room, a glowing little fuse pointing straight out into the world. The sky blurred above them, thinner and thinner the closer morning came, with spit and drooping eyelids as butterflies thronged between ears of corn and horses ran in circles out in the paddock as if the hooves striking the ground, the gentle light, were weaving them into the landscape of dreams. Brynhild just sank deeper into the mattress while the light melted between the treetops and spanned the window frame. The thin hours disappeared without her noticing, the blink of an eye, the seconds, no way to keep up with them, the traitorous soft skin, everywhere unresisting. The creek burbled far away, flies bounced off the windowpane. She heard reins snapping somewhere in front of the house as harnesses were tightened under horses' warm bellies. The days always started like this, all by themselves, sweaty and warm and alone with a sound from the farthest corner of the world. The sound got louder and louder and before she knew it she had to get up and make breakfast and coffee for the masters. Brynhild did it all, so quiet, seventeen, glowing, no one would know what she'd done in the late hours of the night. She wiped down the kitchen counter as fast as she could, gave the floor a quick sweep, put the coffee on, took out cups and plates, set out sausage and eggs, cheese and bread. Her stomach lurched. She was filled with this melting hot world. The dishwater burning hot between her fingers, everything so smooth and scalding on her skin. Seventeen years old with a hot mouth open wide in the middle of the nothingness, seventeen and in a total panic, Brynhild blinked but the colors only pushed deeper into her eyes. Every cell in her body wanted him. There was no doubt about it, happiness and heat filled every crack in her body, Brynhild felt almost drunk as she stood there at the kitchen counter, pulse pounding and rebounding off the walls. She looked out at the pasture. Butterflies flickered just above the ground. She watched them, tracked the wings, tried to count the wing beats but they were fluttering too fast. Time was a heavy pulse behind her eyes. Everything piled up, layer on layer behind her eyes, skinny little legs stabbing right through her irises. It was a mess. Brynhild was seventeen, face-first, open all the way down.

These nights and these mornings, the transitions, the thin blue hours. The sunlight always followed the frame and warmed her face before finding its way to all the small details. Every time she opened her eyes it was just as brutal—the wet panties on the floor, the pale skin alongside her upper arms, his open mouth, the sap trickling from the woodwork. It was grotesque. She lay totally still, this yearning from the depths, a hand on her heart. She didn't understand where it all came from. All the blurry passings back and forth, this aquatic light every single time. Eternal shimmer in the twilight. Brynhild started to understand, this hard and soft were just two sides of the same coin, the shadows and the longings went hand in hand, she just had to turn the other cheek and stay alert, light a candle when night came. The wet panties on the floor, what was the difference really between them and a burning heart? The flame of the paraffin candle flickered, Brynhild felt it with perfect clarity, her heart beating so hard she could barely breathe, the darkness was exactly the same as the light, just as sinful, just as pure.

The days rose up to meet her with a kind of looming silence. God's creation, in its entirety, this butter-yellow light, the shadows on the mattress jabbing into her eyes, this dripping life, the inside and outside of a human life sticking to her fingers. She sat up and looked out the window. The wind was pushing the clouds along and shadows slid across the mattress like looming reminders of everything she'd done the night before. Like they were tapping their fingers on the sheets saying *Look at this!* An encapsulation of all the nights, all the movements that had been forced out of her, she felt the twitching in his body, how he came with his whole self. The new smell clambered into her nostrils, semen and orgasm following the same path as sun and his wide white smile. Straight from the sun. Straight from God. Straight into her eye.

Brynhild waited inside the story and that's what this was all about. Everything crowding round making it all so difficult, everything coming right up next to everything else, all of that in addition to her and Firstborn and the warm mattress, in addition to his body, light and sky, air and dirt, flame and paraffin. In addition to everything she already had and was. She'd been told so many times that she had to know her place, know where she stood, accept her fate. And yet there really was something pushing Brynhild backward and forward at the same time, and she really did stay as still as she could but something was making its way through her guts and insides, between what she saw and felt and what was part of her skin, stuck on her body, between the glass she drank from and the glass she served everyone else. It was perfectly clear, she saw with her own two eyes everything that came between Firstborn and her, between the visible and the invisible, between rich and poor, between where her skin was thickest and where it was thinnest and soft and smooth and almost everything was too much. It was all jammed into the spaces between, it settled into the hollow of her throat and melted into her skin and turned into a gentle rocking of hips, a quiet movement making it impossible for Brynhild to stand perfectly still no matter how hard she tried.

In church Brynhild felt the warmth from the pew radiating up into her thighs, the butter-yellow light burned in her throat and she prayed as hard as she could every night. She felt it, she saw it in the mirror, the little shadow under her chin when she lowered her head, the space between her hands when she carefully folded them to her chest. She felt it in her face. She had so much to give but it was like her eyes were full now and she couldn't tell anything apart anymore, the shadows were everywhere and her breath couldn't find a way out. She carried out her tasks, sloppy, shaking, constantly drying her hands on her apron. She felt only this, all of it gathering in her clasped hands, all of it rocking inside her, the desperate prayers.

13

Brynhild was a little harp and all her strings were vibrating at once. She brushed her lips with her fingers as often as she could, it would turn out later that her heart-shaped little face would be capable of anything, the force in her spine radiated out into her body. The enormous pressure inside her was too much, she had no chance, everything trying to hold it all back strained with all its might. Everything weighed down on her, got dammed up. Her hair stuck to her skin in lines drawn onto her cheekbones and pale freckles, her beautiful skull, everything vibrated, so clear, so strong, as if rising up to the surface from her insides, as if wanting to show the world its delicate structures. Everything, all that there is in a person's life. Brynhild's large blue eyes were sunk in their sockets. She watched every single movement so carefully, she worked so hard at not ending up in a defensive position, not staying alone, but the truth was that her time was running out, both in dreams and in reality.

Seventeen years old, exploding with hormones. A rich man's sweat and her head all the way down in the pillow. A soft kneeling act. Brynhild embraced it, Brynhild wept, *This is all I am, this is all I have*, it was a realization that could fill any little human heart with dark stains. Her small face tried its best to hold tight. She tried to think her way through life, reckon up everything that had happened until this point, but everything filled up her eyes and she stood so timidly, milk-white, dawn-red, like a little child, shimmering tears pouring down into her lap like summer rain. She wiped her face dry with her apron but her hands were always ice-cold, always red, always wet, and there was always more dirty laundry to wash.

Brynhild had been given this whole life, she was supposed to manage it all, but she stood there with her chasm and her arms and life's wild feelings. All of it left up to her. She scrubbed the floors, fetched water from the well, but no matter how many tablecloths she ironed or hens she deboned nothing would ever be the same, the things she'd done went far beyond what someone like her was allowed to do. All this longing, this dripping love-sweat, it stuck to everything she did, these glands in her armpits never stopped stinking. This desire, this big gaping body. How was she supposed to survive it, the pain and the joy, all alive side by side? It fizzed under her tongue and whirled in her chest. These ice-cold hands. Any second now she might lose her grip. She was so scared, so scared of ruining everything. Just the thought that from one moment to the next he might not invite himself in anymore, might not lie down in her bed, might not hold her and kiss her and squeeze her and make her laugh. She'd be all alone, naked, left with a long string of useless moments, and in that case it'd be better if someone did discover and punish them. These nerves, the constant uneasiness, the colors inside her, these ridiculous things inside, instincts and feelings and thoughts like cysts in her body, the huge pictures being painted inside her, they were enormous.

Brynhild was happy, and she cried, this was the paradox she had to live with. Her eyes were like deep lakes in the middle of her face, two light-blue dreams that overflowed and laid down thin stripes on her cheeks. These empty meaningless days, this anguished miserable face, was this the future? Tender feelings escalated in Brynhild, a rising fever-curve, everything she had to endure, everything flowing inside. Shame and intimacy forced its way out of her, always teetering, all the way out on the edge every second. *If God wills it*, she whispered to herself. This must be God's love, the darkest kind, the hottest. She had to have faith in it, her breath sat trapped in her chest, a paralyzing silence lurked in every corner of the house.

Brynhild welcomed it all, she always opened the door with a big smile, and everything came right in, lightning-fast. The times when Firstborn put his hands on her throat, lightning shot through her. *Get on your knees*, he'd said, and she knew it wasn't about evening prayer. His body was so big, mercy didn't exist here, her thoughts dripped scarlet fire, when he told her what he wanted to do to her new mazes of plum juice and fruit pulp unfolded. Seventeen and glowing. All the motions so fast they turned invisible. Impossible to keep up with them. Firstborn found his way to a million magical moments in that attic room. The infinity of these moments eddied through her like newborn galaxies. She had no words for it. This simple naked experience, so easily hurt, so smoldering and intense. Expanses of skin, every single morning, the stinking shame, skin endlessly hot, fear tightening its grip around her neck.

Brynhild couldn't picture any of it without feeling his hand, his big flat palm. Corpse-white, gigantic. And every time Brynhild smiled in the doorway, he might tell her to be quiet even though she wasn't saying anything, and hold her so tight that it almost hurt, and Brynhild thought every time *this can't go on*, but every time it did go on. He let go of her just in time and was nice again and she loved him even more. She ran her fingers over her lips, none of this could stand the light of day, it had all grown too big much too fast, Firstborn kept holding her as the light shrank and went right up to the edge while sweat glistened before her eyes. It was life-threatening. He took her head in his hands, *you're the most beautiful girl I've ever seen.* He peered into the deep lakes in the middle of her face, Brynhild felt how deep he was sinking, how far he wanted to go, how truly hard she had to work to hold back. Tears ran silently down her cheeks, *oh, little Brynhild, what's wrong?* He pulled her close and put his arms around her, holding as hard as he could now that he'd turned so soft.

The sadness in Brynhild moved over to Firstborn, she could see it. There was something in her he couldn't put into words, something transparent he wanted to get to the bottom of. She saw it with perfect clarity, he wanted to go as deep as he could. *This is all I am, this is all I have,* she'd said, but Firstborn interrupted her, his pale hand caressed her cheek, she'd really lost control now. *Big Little B.* She saw everything, there was no doubt about it, this was affectionate, loving, also cold, implacable. But the farther he forced his way into her the more she disappeared, and when he lowered his big body down onto her she vanished completely. Big Little B floated, soared, shining with love, completely gone in the blue hour, in floating soaring nothingness. This was love, this was the purest thing in the world. She was one with creation. She had opened her heart, she was at the pinnacle.

His suntanned skin, strong arms, big hairy chest, she practically knew his every movement by heart, every last little twitch that passed through his body, he would eventually abandon her, leave her entirely alone, she saw it all. The silence, the gentle rocking, the total uncertainty and danger of the situation. Clouds hung low over the hills as if trying to tell her that something had gone wrong, something had changed course. The love had gone deep, that was perfectly obvious, it clung tight with its claws as it had for a while, thin and shiny coating her tongue. She lay there waiting, she pulled the covers up to her chin, she just wanted to let big heavy sleep drag her off to the next best chance, the pale sticky light of day. Brynhild squeezed her eyes shut as hard as she could. But something was now utterly impossible, the abyss rose up before her hot and golden behind her closed eyelids. Time had taken hold inside her, it was growing fingers and toes, a brain, organs. She was pregnant. Nothing could save her now.

A muffled scream butted against her belly, the little light inside her that was going to get bigger and bigger until it made its way out of her all by itself, this was something visible, hard, and terrifying. It would come out with nails and tendons and blood. Brynhild tried to breathe and think and get dressed at the same time but the taste of his mouth inside hers grew and grew, the endlessly hot skin, a baby, nothing came closer. She felt it in every inch of herself, his gigantic body, a new course had been charted. She sat on the edge of the bed soaking wet with terror. She smoothed down her wool skirt, pinned back a lock of her hair. Her face turned completely soft at the thought of this primogenital seed growing inside her. Little explosions all the way up to her collarbone, the craving in her belly. She could hardly breathe. This was love. God's creation. Brynhild looked at the hollow in the mattress, the warm sheets, his impression, the little shadow. Stars poured out her arms, her shining little snake coiled inside her, the purest thing there is between a man and a woman. Nausea filled her to the brim, silently rocking in there between the visible and the invisible.

Brynhild stood in the middle of the room and looked out the window at the farmhouse, making sure to stand far enough back that if he came walking across the yard he wouldn't see her. It had something to do with the transparency of everything, the brutality of the sticky spring light, the secret she was carrying. She saw her reflection in the windowpane, he had gone too far, he'd been looking for what was deepest inside her and hadn't stopped till he found it. It had been so easy to surrender herself, the butter-yellow light had lodged like a ribbon of fat in her throat, the taste of it had blinded her, it was mostly good, not bad. Brynhild shut her eyes and there he was clear as daylight smeared onto the backs of her eyelids. She had something inside her that no one else could see and it was going to strike back at her extra hard. Silence crowded round, blood rushed to her cheeks, the furrow between her eyebrows sat like a weight on the rest of her pale face. Brynhild moved an inch or two farther from the window so that she wouldn't have to see the reflection of her terrified face.

Brynhild stood between the bed and the dresser and wiped away the troubles running down her cheeks. She would have to tell him soon. She would have to stand before him and hold out her arms and tell him that she loved him, that she would carry on the lineage. Brynhild's hands shook. Every hour at the kitchen counter helping the family with breakfast, every second with her fingers in butter and ham and dry bread.

Brynhild held her breath, her body so cold, her joints so stiff, she was dizzy. Every night she folded her hands together. Fear clutched at her heart, every hour it grew bigger and bigger inside her, *dear God*, Brynhild was floating somewhere deep inside herself at the very end of the thread of life.

Brynhild didn't know how it was supposed to feel to be her. Who was she if she wasn't searching for something better? She picked little flowers and put them under her pillow, she tried to hold tight to beauty, gentleness, surprises, life's cunning twists. She let the cold morning air fill the room and aired out the smell of her gaping body. The nausea rose in her throat, how could something so natural be so frightening, she put her corpse-white hand on her belly, if I can't have this then what can I have? The wind blew through the trees, so gentle, *if God wills it*. How could creation be so frightening.

There was something about simple movements, how Big Little B gradually turned into someone else, how she rubbed her belly, how she shifted her weight from side to side, how she had to hold the armrests when she wanted to stand up. She had almost gotten used to it, her body's invisible new changes, her belly's slight curve, her fumbling hands. Every night she sat by herself and listened for everything outside, for a glimmer, an outline, the scope of this story. Listened for everything's lightning-fast maneuvers, everything she couldn't control, everything that disappeared so fast over the edge.

The details, when he was there and when he wasn't, what it was lingering around his mouth waiting for her, a predator's movements, Brynhild sat patiently in her room with her hands on her belly and listened with her curved back. The horses stomped and restlessly pawed at the ground as they got unsaddled. The sky was so big and melting out there, like a soft piece of dark blue silk, much too soft, utterly unbearable. *Dear God*, she lay her hand carefully over her belly button and spread her fingers wide, a whole little world, her hand sticking to her dress, *all this is mine. Lord*, her fingers curled around the edge of her apron, *have mercy on me.*

Brynhild pressed her belly into the mattress, but that didn't make her belly any flatter. Her jaw creaked, her cheeks shone sweaty in the dark. She'd just gone along with everything and now it was still and at the same time changing, all that had been and all that would be. It was like walking in mud. Everything went into this story, she felt something pressing on her chest, the smell of the baby's little head, the sum total of everything, the sacred power, all movements recapitulated in one. The fire in her hips, the gentle rocking. *Lord, have mercy on me*, but the story kept tightening around her, there was less and less room for her insides. The tenderness and how the baby curled up in slow desperate pain, the shining bloodthirsty snake, a wet little warmth in the belly, and then right away the fear would creep up between her shoulder blades.

Fear and love lay like pulsating lines in the landscape, they danced all the way into her eyes in the white morning mist like afterimages of the sun. Birds gathered in flocks and flew through the sky above her; they soared, big and scared, in wide curves before disappearing into the low clouds. It was hard to breathe, lips thick, mouth big, the spit she woke up to every morning. All the things that couldn't bear anything anymore. The dawn-red, the milk-white. The prickling into her eyes, into her ears, she just had to endure it, the stinging in her mouth, the burning in her fingers. She knew it all so well, it shaped her mouth every day and forced it open and got it ready for what was to come, eyes looking down at the floor, the screaming in her neck. The prayer from the pew. A simple motion went through her, eyes bulging at everything around her, these rules that clogged her throat. Brynhild pressed her lips together but it spilled out on both sides, *was this some kind of punishment? Had she not shown enough respect?* Everything pushed its way up her throat, flaming. Where was the dignity in this? Stomach bulging, pulsating from the inside, *please*, Brynhild slapped her mouth, forced her lips together, *what kind of person are you really?* Eyes in the mirror stared back at her. This was an intimacy no one had asked for. She had just gone along with it and he'd lured her all the way out, with both hands. There was no way back.

The day of the party finally came, Brynhild had been looking forward to it for so long, she was going to open her

23

arms and invite him in, a simple gesture, wearing her bright pretty dress and everything. Seventeen with her heart in her throat. She was so gentle, so good. Everything was ready, folded, neatly stacked up in her chest. The evening light got tangled up in her hair and the quivering in her head prickled behind her eyes, up and down the bone of her nose. Everything that had ever pushed into her, into her heart, fought to come out at the same time; she stood there with everything she'd experienced glittering right in the middle of her face. She was so beautiful that summer night, filled with herself right to the brim, as if she'd never done anything else, and right then and there with her skin and her hair and her whole glowing self she was the sum total of everything, the purest of them all. There was not a single dirty thought left in her head. She looked at Firstborn and a single long breath moved through her body. Her craving was so huge. She looked at him. Firstborn with his big blond curls and squeaking boots, with his hands that always knew where they wanted to go. He took a step closer, warm drool flowed along her gums, and he leaned toward her, slowly, with his big soft mouth. Firstborn laughed and Big Little B held her breath. She closed her eyes, balancing with both feet, she searched herself all the way to the edge of her tongue, that shiny little ribbon of fat. Her whole face prickled, *keep an open heart*, she whispered, *please*. He breathed heavily into her ear, *Big Little B*, but his gaze slid right through her toward the treetops behind her. The wind blew a warning but she didn't hear anything except rustling branches. There was no contact, he wasn't there. Unease scrambling up her throat, she smelled liquor on his breath, landowning, rich, elite, quick-tempered. He really was so addicted to his own desire. She looked at the two open buttons on his shirt, her lust was obvious, throbbing, milk-white, dawn-red, while his eyes were swimming in booze. Big Little B took hold of her courage and brought forth what had lain hidden in darkness so long. Her voice shook as the words slipped across her lips, *I'm going to have a baby.* Her heart pounded like in a nightmare, she felt it with perfect clarity, there is nothing left after this.

Firstborn had been standing and looking at her for a while, somehow absently, now he turned his whole body toward her. Something was wrong, she heard the beating of birds' wings, their deadly fear in the lingering silence. His look was streaked black, absent, perfectly flat. The slanting movement, the streak of light, the depths of them both, she couldn't take her words back. The distance between them was perfect, he had tensed his body from stomach to shoulder and from the thigh down and he put all his strength into one simple movement. Everything was transparent, she saw it in him, this was the horrible moment before her body hit the ground. His foot hit her stomach, the leather boot hit the target. Then and there the world collapsed, lightning flashed through her, it was as if she had never existed.

The darkness opened like a drop of ink in a glass of water, it spread silently, filling her all the way up to the edge of her eyelids until not a single thought was left. Firstborn had walked away, just left her lying there with the taste of dirt in her mouth. Brynhild, so gentle and good, so good and so alone that Firstborn had taken a chance, she'd either survive or she wouldn't, what did he know. He had gone as deep as he could and now there was nothing left, one silent moment and he'd crushed her. The summer breeze slipped through the branches, warmly caressed her face, it pushed her head down into the dirt, all while whispering gently, discreetly, *you can die now.*

Tears flooded every gap inside her, speechlessness lay in every fold. But Brynhild wasn't dead, she heard the river cry, she felt the marks the ground had left on her cheek. She had lost all feeling in her arms and legs. He had stood right next to her, utterly implacable, he'd taken what he wanted; she couldn't get up, she lay there with her chasm, wide open, exposed to the bone. A painful kneeling ceremony. The silent shriek filled the air around her, her face had changed and now was trying desperately to find its way back to itself. It was a dying movement, a scornful face in static tension. The moon came out from behind the clouds and settled between the trees where she was lying with what remained of a rich man's sweat in her hands, where the pale glow of a life had started and ended in the same second. Big Little B lay there in the dusk with the moonlight on her face, the blue hours like vicious bruises pooling under her skin. The warm wind that had made her blood rush lingered up in the treetops, staring calmly down at her.

I T WAS VERY STRANGE how weightlessly she was floating inside herself. A wide white smile. A moment of closeness. Something had gotten out of hand. The silence filled her with a calm golden light, very soft for a few seconds before the pressure came down from above. It slammed down, broke off, oblivion couldn't carve out enough space, and the moment disappeared as quickly as it had come. Sensations of choking welled up inside her, a hissing voice jammed itself between the sweat and the nightmares, she could still feel him deep inside. This body, full of tears, empty of words, it had been given what it asked for—everything. The heart really did have to carry its own weight. The sky was dark yellow above Rødde Farm, above Stjørdal, flowing with perfect clarity, melting over her heart, chest pounding weakly while words tickled against her ribcage, *what kind of person are you?* She couldn't breathe. It was no bigger than that, but no smaller than that either. This was a young body's breaking point, curse and blessing. Belly and womb bled empty. Big Little B lay there like a toothless mouth, no longer waiting inside the story, she had been pulled out of the story like someone with no memory while the days only got darker and shorter.

Brynhild felt the cold against her skin. Everything there was dammed up with her crying, she kept her mouth shut and tried to swallow but acid reflux stung her gums. The time it took to separate longings from memories, one from the other, it was pathetic, weak. Brynhild looked down at her red hands, there was no strength left in them. Insomnia sat in heavy sallow rings under her eyes, blue and gray as if sheathing something powerless. Why had this happened to her, of all people? Brynhild stood up, slowly got dressed, tied her apron tight, and washed in hot water until her hands were almost scalded. Her brain worked to sustain and manage everything, to make life worth living, but now it was like every day someone was skating over her heart with sharp blades. She had to bear it, the leftover food and the smell and the color in the corner of her eye. He remained inside her like a constant inflammation; love had killed all it could.

The days at Rødde Farm meant nothing now and Brynhild had to go home. To the Størset property, to mom and dad and the six sheep up on the hill. Her little room waited in total darkness and the farm breathed the same way it had all along, gathered into one big body, a large farm bound together by generations, a protective chain of muscle, skin, and bone. Somewhere she didn't belong. Brynhild had washed the bedsheets and the work clothes, she carefully undid the clothespins, took everything off the line, folded it neatly, and lay it on the bed next to the apron. She picked up the small suitcase with her things and walked carefully down from the attic. The cold air hit her in the face when she got outside. Every step felt so brutal, she had to just think don't think, but it took everything she had and now she needed to go home. Brynhild walked across the yard, taking little careful steps. The light hung overhead, big and heavy as lead, she hadn't managed to do what she should have, it took too much. She pressed her lips together; she wasn't going to leave a single gap open. With silent footsteps she started down the long way home, she didn't have to stop and turn around. Her thighs chafed, she was dressed in wool, but she was freezing to the bone.

NO ONE SAID
LIFE WAS EASY

THE STØRSET PROPERTY

B RYNHILD HAD BEEN GIVEN this whole life. She had to live it all, had to manage everything, but now there was nothing left and she lay curled up facing the wall, a black hole, sucking everything in. Her mother came through the doorway, light flooded in from the window behind her as she stood holding the bowl of washing water, all that strangeness at a blinding angle. A kind of angel. Brynhild looked at her, everything in her mother so quiet, belated, dim and blurry, that wretched filthy life that couldn't help anyone. It was like the colors had been sucked out of her. Brynhild felt the warm cloth against her skin, the dripping water on her neck, her eyelids were so heavy. Something had become impossible, it was obvious—this angel came with a warning. *To the pure all is pure*, but Brynhild was not pure and she had to get rid of all this powerlessness, all she'd promised, all the blood, all the fear. The prayer was painful to the touch inside her light cotton dress, the strongest force cut through her skin, the deepest longing. Her own desperate cries. All worthless now. It all had to go, but it didn't go, and there in bed her skin was scrubbed red. The little bed where she'd lain since she was a newborn with her arms sticking straight out into the room, completely defenseless. Brynhild had met the gaze of every stranger who picked her up. Cold cheek against a warm body, big smile, friendly eyes resting on her. The eternal taste of dirt in the mouth. All stiff in a white nightgown, a proof of God screaming, *what kind of person are you?* Brynhild couldn't answer for anyone, she was as defenseless as life itself. What had forced its way into her wouldn't let go. The merciless screaming, the shameful skin. The big open world. She was soaking wet, freezing to the bone, and she felt the nausea, the meaninglessness trickling down the walls.

Brynhild had to go away, as far from this sad place as humanly possible. This hard black soil where birds never landed, this village where God saved not one living soul. Where God left her freezing cold against the drafty wall, where everyone got sick and caught fevers and drowned in the vicious white snow. There was no mercy here, no forgiveness, only cold and rot and mice in the walls. The Atlantic Ocean was sparkling somewhere out there, she had heard of it and she had to believe in it, but Big Little B just wanted to disappear, fade into nothing, like the eternal blue point in the middle of the flame. Brynhild felt the ringing in her ears, a prickling in front of her eyes, the life being pulled out of her body, *if God can still see*, but the world said nothing. The darkness and silence drowned out everything else. There was nothing divine about this, it was cheap and tacky, kneeling on the dirt floor, dirty hands shoveling food into mouths, the craving in her belly that was nothing but hunger gnawing at her ribs. No wide smile, no moment of closeness.

A WEAK HISS drifted out along the horizon, light slipped along the edge like a heavy eyelid. Brynhild dragged the suitcase up the gangway, walked one step after another through the big gray sheet of nothingness. Firstborn lay inside her like a hundred symptoms, but if he could turn his back and leave then why couldn't she. She tried to give it shape, make room for a big streak of light all the way to the back of her mouth, God's eternal light, the waiting, a single big fumbling, *who are you really?* Brynhild was dragging everything she owned on board the boat, this was all she was, and he had taken it. She had let him be the greatest, at the very top, and he had taken everything she gave him and played God. There was no more spit left to drool, no more saliva stains on her face to wipe away. No hope left for sentimentality. The flashing water beat against the current, she closed her mouth and stayed standing on deck till the Atlantic Ocean filled her and the waves boiled in her eyes, until he was behind her like a worldview cracked and broken.

The strip of coast disappeared into the sea like a sticky gray mass of something old; waves foamed behind the boat in a long line. She stood there with froth at the corners of her mouth and bruises behind her eyes. The masses of water were so strong, they plowed ahead, a voracious and passive will filled Brynhild and the farther out to sea they went the clearer it got, it was a Trøndelag nightmare, a sad summary, her smooth face, a blank center with nothing in front or behind.

The sun burned into her face and the ship moved beneath her like a big heavy animal, bursting from top to bottom, crowded with people. Up on deck her eyes twinkled like two silver coins as the light played on waves whipped white. Heat filled her head and the nausea crept all the way out to her fingertips, her pulse pounded in her temples. Her brown hair stuck to her forehead; disgust, dizziness, all the people around her full of hope, everything crawling in, the light twisting brighter and brighter into her eye sockets, she felt her skin pushing her eyes deeper and deeper into her skull. Then the ship listed to one side and she lost her balance and woke up again. She'd slipped. It was perfectly obvious and her stomach's menacing vibrations lay shapeless and wet before her. The tenderness, broken and scattered, right there. She wrapped her coat closer around her body, stood there with wool socks stuffed into boots she'd laced so tight her feet hurt, and that was the first time Brynhild saw the sea, the white eye of the storm, always before her like the abyss in another person. There was nowhere to rest, nowhere to go, a thousand worn-out questions in the middle of the ocean. She was surrounded. All this that could kill and crush her, that could swallow her up and fill her throat with suffocating white foam. Intense colors whipped ahead in the waves, settled into her eyes, right there, her face was so bright confronting the dark water. As she went down below deck she heard the sick bodies thudding against the walls. The infected were stowed away in their own cabins so their hands wouldn't touch anyone. They weren't to drag anyone else down into the undertow with them. Waves crashed over the deck, her face was all white. Fever boiling in her body, skin hotter than seemed possible, on edge all the time, on the verge, she held tight as hard as she could as the sky gathered strength again. It was supposed to take two weeks, she and the ship both balanced on a deadly edge. Every morning the ship was floating in the mist, the white dawn. The sky stuck to her eyes, the truth clear and shining before her. Brynhild had to bear it. No miracles came, no angels; for almost the whole crossing she stood out on deck without talking to a single living soul. She had tied her mother's old woolen shawl over her hair, a cry quivered inside her cheek, a hundred broken thoughts lay scattered over everything, the never-ending taste of dirt, God said not a word. The sun shone hard, thin clear sea air splashed in her lungs, seagulls gathered above the boat in white clouds of screams, everything chirping in her ears, slowly swaying. She couldn't do it, it was unbearable, the amount of light was too harsh for her skin with white freckles, the contours of a new color, the wood beneath her fingers, too many flashing surfaces, more and more birds' eyes and birds' wings, all the fluttering inside her pupils, the flickering, the fibers in her skin, the blood vessels in her eyes, the thin red lines, everything just getting bigger and bigger, light pouring down like rain and getting everywhere, it was impossible, but then the coastline rose up before her. Brynhild squinted in disbelief, her eyes flashed, the boat glided calmly into port. The Statue of Liberty stood there so tall with a torch glowing at the very top.

EVERYONE
ALWAYS LOVES
SOMEONE ELSE

B RYNHILD DRAGGED the suitcase onto the train. In the
dusk her hands were like white skeleton hands and her
bones, that eternal fragile structure always trying to hold a
person upright, shone through her skin under the streetlamps.
Moments of closeness, belief in something bigger than herself, Brynhild had to move on, she had to get to Chicago, she
had to find her way on her own, that's what Nellie had said,
one step at a time, she had to watch her money too, watch the
door and the stairs and the compartment, she had to carry
the suitcase on board and not let it out of her sight. Then,
only then, could she lean back and watch the train slip farther
and farther into the country, see how it swallowed up mile
after mile, how the forests and the prairies melted together
in the middle, how everything was bigger, wider, and longer
over here. Nellie and her husband had promised to take her
in. Nellie had written about all this, how Brynhild had to
take the train and not talk to anyone, how the lakes could

be so calm, Nellie had written about lakes big as oceans, beautiful, icy blue, filled to the brim. Michigan, Superior, Huron, Ontario, and Erie, untouched by human hands, there were no words for it, everything really was bigger and more beautiful, not snaking little arms of fjords like back home, the lakes here lay in the landscape like eyes filled with tears. Brynhild had never seen so much water before she set foot aboard the boat. Brynhild sat with her suitcase right next to her, her weeks on the ocean still in her body, that gentle rocking there were no words for. She had finally reached the other side, finally, and she slid farther and farther in, the train drilling its way through the forest and hope welling up in her sensitive face. Darkness flooded out between the trees. She rested her forehead against the cold train window, pupils fluttering at everything outside, everything melting together before her eyes. The land was fertile, that's what everyone said, they said you could get rich practically over-night, the natural resources were endless, there were lots of Norwegians, lots of husbands, everything could be created anew and so, so much better. She could see it all with her naked eye, there was no doubt about it—everyone here could have as much as they wanted. Her eyes were drawn to the water between the trees, to everything that vanished between the tree trunks and never came out again, it glittered far away in there somewhere, but the primeval forest pricked into her eyes, hope feverishly hammered in her chest.

The train slid into the platform and the station glowed in the light of the setting sun. Brynhild held her money tight in her pocket and almost started crying when she saw her sister waving her arms amid the mass of people, she stretched up on her toes as high as she could and her older sister Nellie pushed her way through the crowd. Time whispered so softly in Brynhild as she stood there with both feet on the platform. But American soil was like Norwegian soil, she couldn't feel any difference. She squinted, the sun painted Lake Michigan yellow, and her sister was so beautiful in the melting light, *Brynni, my girl!* Nellie cried. When Brynhild heard her name so loud and clear it was like something inside her burst for a millisecond, she took a deep breath as if in prayer. *This is all I am, this is all I have*, then Nellie pulled her close and hugged her. Nellie's body was so soft and warm, she smelled so good and so clean, and Brynhild leaned all the way in, she held tight and Nellie didn't let go. There was something about the insight Brynhild had then and there in Nellie's arms that turned everything upside down—the wild liberation, this sudden feeling, she just wanted to hold Nellie tight and never let go. Brynhild felt the breath unfold in her body, like butterfly wings carrying her soul out her mouth, as if breath was finally reaching her lungs.

Nellie had already gotten Brynhild a job as a maid with some friends of the family, as a seamstress when they needed extra hands. Clearly there was a life to be had here. She didn't need to go back, she could just lean in, take a dip in the lake, embrace everything Nellie gave her. But you couldn't sit still here, pale Norwegian skin alongside the thin threads of everything. What she had inside her obviously had to all come out as soon as it could. Brynhild carried the world's cruelty right under her skin, but also the world's beauty. Brynhild put the silver thread in her mouth and into the needle and let it slide through the fabric for so many hours every day, it left sparkling little stitches in the fabric. But it felt like a flicker belonging to the old world, settling down over her face and paralyzing her. The paralysis spread through her whole body. She took a breath as if trying to make herself taller, lighter, easier, like her body was both willing to and begging to become someone else, but powerlessness just sat in her work apron and shone up at her, it spat in her face, all by itself, she had to take what was given to her and wrap it around her waist. The whole thing was an insult, a joke. But she had to keep at it, she couldn't say no, what else was she going to do and Nellie was standing there with her questioning face the whole time as if just waiting for Brynhild to tell her more juicy secrets from the old country. Like she enjoyed it. So many moments when the thread broke in two, when it slipped and broke in the middle and was torn and ugly, so many problems, all the times she couldn't bear to pull it up through the fabric again, all those dresses, all those petticoats, Brynhild wanted things to just look nice, why couldn't they just look nice? Brynhild tried everything she could, she tried with everything she had, to make things prettier than they'd ever been and she started with the easiest thing and changed her name to Bella. And it almost happened, she almost became more beautiful, she almost changed completely, all by herself, she almost turned into a totally new person, it was like her face was a little smoother even, a little less recognizable. Bella picked up an eyelash that had come loose and was lying on Nellie's velvety cheek, *there's no reason to hold back*, she told Nellie, *yes, well, it's just a matter of wanting something enough, Brynni*, Nellie said. *My name is Bella now*, Bella said bluntly, and she blew the dark little eyelash into the wind.

It was so beautiful over here, and every morning a strange mist hung in the air around Nellie's house by the water, gray and cautious, floating over the lake and the rooftops with a sort of glimmer of darkness. Bella stared at everything around her, at the furniture in the living room, the fog floated so low that all she could see out the window was the water and the birds, she couldn't hear a thing, she saw only a wide, motionless surface of water far away. It was nicer than it had been, there was no doubt about it, and at night waterlilies came into view and bobbed on the water's little ripples. They floated like glowing lanterns in the evening darkness, swam straight toward where she stood deep inside

Nellie's living room. Bella felt the fundamental movement of existence, rocking, powerful. Words were too small and her future found her everywhere, *if God wills it*, the sounds of the water lapped. She closed her eyes, the taste of salt clung to her lips, her jaw tightened till it was rock hard.

There was something about the simple movements that everyday life was filled with now. Bella learned how to quickly shift a piece of fabric with nimble elbows, finish a seam, use scissors, cut splits, stick pins into pincushions, carry out the tailor's orders, punch out and punch in. But every time she saw the fabric tear between her hands, always on the verge of falling apart, the idea that someone would give her a pair of scissors felt so brutal. There was something about the silence that went with this kind of work, about the sharp shiny blades and how they slid through smooth fabric. No resistance at all, like a hot knife through butter, how could the cloth be so soft and the scissors so hard? Her eyes felt full of tears. Everything swooned and teetered around her, merged with the mist and the heat of her body every morning, and Bella's only wish was to find some balance, find someone who could hold her, someone who loved unconditionally, like Nellie but without that questioning face. She sat with the scissors in one hand and the silver thread and dress fabric in the other. Blood surged so powerfully through her, she felt it trickle, she filled her arms so full with the smooth fabrics and silky movements but always her doubt remained, every night she came home and ate the cold dinner Nellie had set aside for her. Nellie had left the first chance she got, left her there in the brown wet moor and never looked back. Nellie had her own family now, a big house and kids of her own, a flicker of another world that refused to let her in. This is all I have, Bella knew. This really is everything.

Brynhild had become Bella, she was a new person, but anything given to her could also be taken away, and the romance and the beautiful light over Lake Michigan was absolutely horrible, she felt like she was about to throw up. The fabrics lay folded in thick rolls that she piled against the wall—dusty rose, white, ocher, orange. But nothing resonated, none of what she saw reflected what was inside her. Inside her all was gray, a blank indifferent fog. You need to find yourself in your surroundings before you can find yourself within yourself, but no matter how beautifully the mist settled over the lake at dusk or dawn or how gently the waves or muscles sang within her it was pure dumb luck that she didn't take everything she had patched together and rip it to pieces.

The hot muggy air swelled above the water. Lake Michigan was laughing at her with its little stinging insect sounds. Things out there found not a single echo inside her, not in her body, not in her brain, absolutely not in her heart. Bella sat there with her scissors and a small, unclear craving in her belly—anyone could get as much as they wanted over here but she didn't want anything, there were no nuances, just a sad desire, a sad heavy longing she poked at during the night. She was sitting with a blood-red roll of fabric and playing with the tips of the scissors, she saw it all with perfect clarity. The beauty was deadly and there was something there, something massive, murky, unforgivable. Bella found herself in a big, wide-open world but she couldn't trust herself anymore. What had she actually destroyed? These movements, these intentions, *who are you really?* Her body extended out in different directions, she didn't understand it, so flat and paralyzing on one side, so gluttonous and quick to anger on the other. Bella was utterly defenseless, utterly left to fend for herself with the whole prairie hammering in her chest. Sharp metal slid through fabric, everything was so dangerous if only she wanted it to be. She sat every day in her chair with a claw clenched in her back and scissors in her lap, full of impotence, blood, and urine. She took her head in her hands. That battered head, the pressure behind her eyes, it never stopped, the same memory exploded and trickled to the ground every time, the melting black light spread into every nook and cranny, with thorns up in her face, the great hand of God lifted her up, through the night, through the clouds, into the light, until she saw the sandy riverbed, all that was left on the ground below, running in among the trees to the foul-smelling black pool. God, the great movement, hadn't forgotten her, he just wanted her to remember precisely what had happened.

Bella found herself in a different time zone, more confrontational, it was like the light woke up more ferocious here. It attacked from all sides at once. As if God's presence was stronger here and the story of creation was still taking shape. The light shone with a kind of aggression as if God was asking to be tested, faith had to be put on trial, people had to figure things out for themselves. A hard push from all sides, the colors swirled before her bloodshot eyes. She touched her mouth, *this is how I am*. Fingers brushed her lips, *this is my world*. It took strength to hold back. Bella felt the pressure behind her eyes, memories kept trickling into her mouth and filling her with their syrupy light, there was no doubt about it, everything was ripping apart between her fingers. Lake Michigan swelled and whispered, *this is what God is*.

The times Bella was able to hold on to a feeling she spent the whole day either in the pew or in the study. She tried to lure her thoughts into her mouth so that she could get closer to an explanation; she tried to hook the thoughts onto words and hold them tight long enough to at least explain her despair to Nellie, but the thought would slip away and Bella would forget what she had been thinking or feeling. Everything could stay inside her so blank and lifeless, so warm and inaccessible. She stared at Nellie's beautiful children,

51

who always had to be persuaded to come along to church on Sunday, every single time, it took so long, waiting in the hall, all dressed up, in tight shoes, it was always too long for Bella to understand anything and drops of sweat would start to trickle out from under her hat. Nellie almost had to force them to go with Bella. Didn't they like her? What didn't she understand? It was as if all the food she had ever eaten was growing in her mouth, cream and sugar clogging her throat and everyone expecting so much more from her than she could ever give. Maybe she didn't like them that much either, but they were family, weren't they? She took off her gloves and carefully paged through the children's Bible on the dresser in the hall, and when the children finally marched up she looked at them and whispered, so that Nellie couldn't hear, *God doesn't forgive anyone.*

Bella tried to let her shoulders relax in the sight of God and she sat down in the pew, lowered her head, folded her hands, took a deep breath. The church had dazzled her the first time she saw it, its walls so white, so big, it stood behind a makeshift picket fence that held both God and the homeland in one and the same gesture, a place where beliefs looked for community and the community looked toward Norway. The Norwegian Synod in the dark spruce forest, it was like a mirror image of everything back home, the cliffs plunging down into the lakes, the pine trees, the ice-cold water. *Dear God*, Bella closed her eyes and sank as deep as she could, she tensed her hands tight in her lap and felt warmth from the wood, you could really live a whole life searching for forgiveness, she prayed as hard as she could even if the words sat almost lifeless on her tongue, luckily the services were still held in Norwegian. Every now and then the children crawled right up onto her in the pew and fell asleep in her lap, and then something stirred inside her, something so pure and innocent, she felt the warmth of the sleeping children's bodies and ran her fingers through their curly hair, so golden, so soft and pure and special. Her whole body felt calm, the holiest thing in the whole wide world lay right there, nestled in her lap where it should be, safe and sound, how could they not love her? How could they not love all of this? Everything was so stripped bare, she felt the sunlight through the window warming her face, so this was really what love is. She felt it so clearly. Sacred power. Absolute purity.

Bella had access to the children, but that was it. She had not been able to meet people or find any male company, any good friends. Nothing ever loosened up, there was always something that became too much, someone who stared a little too long with empty eyes and a suggestive leer in the corners of his mouth, glaring Norwegian men who'd left everything they came from for a wet little plot of land and who thought she would become their wife. Every single Sunday a whole small village of lost men turned up on the church steps. The women with their pious expressions tried to take in the pastor's sermons and while Bella squeezed her folded hands and stared down at her lap she could feel the grinning eyes on the back of her neck. She twisted a lock of hair around her finger and tried to take it all in, the light coming in through the window, the little head in her lap, God's forgiveness. An embroidered tapestry hung high up near the ceiling above the baptismal font, its squiggly writing flowed down toward the communion table, *The Lord our God is a consuming fire*, the words were executed so gracefully with both flowers and flames winding around the letters, this was true beauty. Bella repeated the words to herself but felt no purification. She sat there among the unfaithful, everyone just pretending, all the farmers trying to live their lives with their wheat and their potatoes and their endless fields of corn. Every night Bella sat with the Bible in her lap and turned her gaze to the sky. There were so many stars out here on the prairie, so much sky, God truly was great. *The Lord our God is a consuming fire*, she repeated, *Lord, if you still see me, what do you want me to do?* The air was packed tighter and tighter around her head. She blew her nose into her sister's embroidered handkerchief then folded it up nicely and put it back in her skirt pocket.

Bella couldn't do it. Every morning her room was filled with soft drowsiness, the sweet smell that awakens in a person before anything else, a strange layer of something that made its way into her nightmares and kept her dreams hidden so far away that she felt nothing but a sort of blurry discomfort every time she saw the children at the breakfast table. It didn't work though. Sleep brought out the old black sweat in her, the kind that dripped behind her eyelids and smelled worse than anything. That made everything grow much too big too fast. That made everything difficult and disgusting. The nightgown clung to the tip, mother's milk flowed yellow and sickly from her breasts, rage rose up in force. Everything was so blue and black—in her dreams she saw herself standing between the dresser, and the bed totally naked in all that dark blue, as it pushed forward, she brought it out with both hands, the beginning the middle and the end, she was folding her hands tightly as if in prayer and straining until blood vessels burst in the children's eyes. Her heart was racing as hard as it could and the sweat came in big dark drops. She woke up scared to death. She had to sit up on the edge of the bed, she ran her fingers over the pillowcase. She couldn't help it, every single time she closed her eyes she conjured up a soft little hell.

Our Father, who art in heaven. Hallowed be thy name, everything lay stuck to her neck, her eyes lay deep in there somewhere, water flowed under her arms, *thy will be done, dear God, who art in heaven, can you forgive me soon?* Bella let the words stream almost silently from her lips at the breakfast table, *lead us not into temptation.* She took a bite of the dry bread and met

Nellie's gaze over their coffee cups. Nellie desperately trying to get the children to bless the porridge before they shoveled it down their throats, Nellie who tried to make them better than they really were.

Bella just was, and it wasn't enough, and she tried to be a God-fearing person in this new world, thinking new thoughts among the lakes and the sounds of the water. Nellie would often come up to her with a small cup of tea and tell her that the food would be ready soon, *I think you have a nervous condition,* Nellie might also say when she saw Bella's white face praying down at the floor, her clenched fists raised over her head, *there's treatment for that, you know.* But this had nothing to do with nerves, Nellie had to realize that, sitting on the living room floor in a pale-yellow silk dress and raising her children to think they were better than everybody else, *Aunt Bella's just a little anxious.* Bella sat and watched them as the honeybees and bumblebees flew in from the garden and made a kind of faint organ music with their buzzing, Bella stared into the world with its caresses and promises, she searched for meaning in the words that flowed from her tongue, she tried to learn all the nuances of this new language, but the days went by and Bella lost her grip. Bella sat quietly in her corner, now at the edge of the bed, now pleading with her forehead on the bedroom floor, chewing slowly at the kitchen table with the light throbbing in front of her face, *deliver us from evil,* from the blank and lifeless. The voices by the lakes blended with the hum of the bees from the garden and the sound of Nellie's sad life. The sun's glare on the yellow silk dress whispered to Bella, everything out there whispered to Bella, the church spires stuck straight up and pierced the sky until the starlight ran out and streamed down her hair, the night crept over her and her brain opened like an old wound and coaxed her, in the coldest voice it had, caressing her face, *it must hurt to remember the people who didn't want you?*

Bella felt sensations of vomiting, everything raced along at tremendous speed and she was either too slow or too close, the nuances disappeared and she couldn't understand anything except what was totally obvious. The simple words in a completely different language, *yes* and *no*, kept her afloat; the piety and the beauty bore the same unwavering faith; she saw the children playing together in the living room, created by the purest light, but she couldn't make them do anything they didn't want to do. The blank lifeless tongue filled her with a tremendous sorrow she felt in her whole chest, *this is my world.*

Bella ate small spoonfuls of Nellie's porridge. She tried to do everything as honorably as she could, but every time she sat there and looked at the salty butter melting in the middle, the bright point disappearing into the gray mud, there was a kind of hope too, a promise that something was going to change. She had to believe in it, this shining fat right in front of her, she had to believe, Bella stared down into the butter and felt something push against her leg. The children's small house cat came creeping timidly out from under the sofa. Bella bent down to pick it up and it licked her face right away. All things would pass, she felt it, this was a clear sign—the innocence shining up into her face, the innocence that had come looking for her with its slit eyes. Bella peered into the hairy little face and the little cat stared back at her, *now who are you, you little thing?* she asked, her voice sounding fake. Rough tongue across both cheeks, butter and cat hair everywhere, sunlight blinded her and the tongue scraped her down to the cheekbones, there was something completely impossible about this, this hope, this mess, this cat licking her face with its little tongue. This had to be God's way of speaking to her, her jaw creaked, it was so irresistible, much too soft and much too breakable. Bella pressed her lips gently into the soft fur, *now why are you so cute?* Her voice was still just as fake-sounding and her jaw ratcheted tighter, the light was so harsh, Bella was almost drowning. The fur was completely inside Bella's iris and the cat's tail snaked up toward the ceiling and swung from side to side as the cat extended its claws. Everything Bella could get under her eyelids, open eyes, raw mind, it all grew and grew the more she pressed her face into its fur. She felt rapacity seeping out from somewhere, she tightened her grip to keep the cat quiet but it was like it was talking to her from somewhere deep inside her, somewhere denying her what she really wanted, Bella stopped for a second, *what are you waiting for, really?* And she heard it with perfect clarity, coming from somewhere far away, *a miracle*, Bella whispered, *just a little miracle.*

Everything in her life, everything that could have been different—this was the only organized thought Bella had. She put the cat back down on the floor, it slipped out of her grasp and out the open door. She tasted salt and saw a hundred reflections on her retina, bleeding gums, lightning across the sky, *what are you waiting for?* Bella's surroundings only confirmed her inner life as she stood alone in the middle of the room. Nellie and the family's soft breathing, the interconnecting lung of life. Hearing it was intolerable, she put the hot cloth over her face, slowly scratched herself red, but her face was still attached to her head and the mirror showed only the same desperate face it showed every other day. Bella thought about the goodbyes back home, there was nothing honorable about them, no one had become a better person, and Nellie held her children so close as if protecting them from Bella, Bella couldn't let go. Bella counted her blessings and joys on her fingers, but there were neither fingers nor joy left over for anything else. She said her evening prayers and the darkness closed in on all sides, blank and lifeless, shadow under her chin, everything given to you could also be taken away. Bella lay there alone, waiting for God's cleansing fire.

The butterflies out in the garden were singing as if nothing had happened. It was the same in America as in Norway—it didn't matter, the world didn't care about her. Love was what made it possible for anything and everything to exist, she could see that just by looking at her nieces and nephews, but Bella didn't know if there was enough love left, there was something about Nellie's lips, they were oozing something strange. Bella knew it was a very different kind of embrace she needed but Nellie didn't understand anything. And everything flickered like that, treetops swayed heavily back and forth outside the window, wind rustled through the leaves, Bella wiped the drool from her chin, *I don't think Nellie loves me anymore*, she whispered. She ran her hand over her stomach, her navel, the little moles receding farther and farther into her skin, the air was so muggy and stagnant, they were sisters but how exactly were they similar? Loneliness had taken its toll and she looked nothing at all like Nellie. Bella stood in front of the mirror like a big friendly giant, trying to find the love within her. There was something in there, crouching, pale and sickly. Bella stared into life and saw herself lying all alone at the bottom. She felt her scream sink deeper into her chest, it was only a matter of time. All stories end with death, this one too, Bella knew that. But she forgot it when Mads Sørensen walked into the room. She begged and prayed then too, but in a completely different way.

RED SUMMER

M ADS CAME, and he got close a little too fast, lips first, and it startled Bella. She gave Mads Sørensen nothing at first, but then changed her mind and gave him everything. She rested her whole chin on his shoulder and opened her mouth a little so he could peek inside. She stood there, trying her best, like an open cathedral door leading into the darkness, there was something so ready inside her, a flash of insight, it tried to hide but she focused all her attention on it, this vision of something new, she almost stood on her tiptoes hanging by her chin. Mads was all dressed up and she heard his lungs murmuring through his mouth, a well-tuned system of trembling movements. It didn't matter why it was Mads who came or why he stayed so long but his coming changed everything, and now Bella was so tight and soft at the same time, her brain, her thoughts, she felt the knowledge in her spine, love had found her at last. Bella ran her fingers over her dark brown braids hanging down over each shoulder, how they twisted, every last little braid—it was an art to find the balance, how tight to braid it without hurting anywhere, the long-awaited moment when everything was just as it should be, the painful and the beautiful together. It seemed like an impossible balancing act, separating the anticipation from the pain, the inside from the outside, and it was hard enough for Bella to open up, she didn't know how to close up again, but she tried to be as concrete as she could without handing herself over to Mads. And so she stood with mouth half open while the sun, the wind, and the time trickled by and split into seconds and hours. The miracle had come, it was perfectly obvious, and so this was how it was, Mads Sørensen strolling around carefree with burning lust in his eyes. Like a drooling dog he circled her. Beauty always looks like destruction, beauty always could be destruction, she had to accept that.

It would have been impossible to hold anything back. Mads had kissed her neck and stroked her belly and Bella couldn't take it anymore, she had fallen back on the bed and opened her heart and spread her legs all at once. Mads said everything she'd been longing to hear since forever, *you've been living in a bad dream, baby*, the hairs on her arms stood on end, someone had finally found her. She blinked away a tear. The mattress creaked beneath them and she felt herself again staring down into the darkness of her guts, she sank deeper, but Mads just repeated her movements and seemed totally untouched by the whole thing, *my baby*. Bella felt the vibrations from his voice but couldn't see him as long as he was behind her. The words rolled off his tongue so easily and tickled her back and settled into the little curls at her hairline, *I'm going to cry*, Bella whispered as she lay face down on the pillow, the lump in her throat only getting bigger, *this is what love looks like*, Mads said, *I promise you, baby*. A huge wave crashed over her one last time and Bella's voice reached out toward him, *baby, please*. The steel springs of the mattress compressed under the weight of the two of them, the weight of one lone person surrendering completely to another.

Mads slept, his chest rising and falling as if it had never done anything else, as if it breathed only for her. Bella wiped her mouth and lay there staring at him, so easily accessible, his whole being, this whole person, it surpassed all understanding. The night pressed up close to the window and Bella felt the silence on her body. She sat up carefully so as not to wake him and opened the Bible on her lap, leafed a little through the thin pages, but only got impatient and restless. Bella had to believe in the God she knew, in what her heart could hold, in what Mads could fill. She had to believe that she was capable of a hundred new experiences, a whole new life if she wanted; she stared out at the garden but there was nothing to see. The house was floating in the dark. She put the Bible down on the nightstand, this is love, *my baby*, she repeated the words exactly as he'd said them. Like a moth to the flame, that's what I am, *my baby*. A burnt little body folded under the covers, sore all over, totally naked, a firefly in the dark. The remnants of an abandoned dream took refuge in her body and she suddenly felt so weightless, she pressed herself against Mads until everything flickered before her eyes.

Mads Sørensen had knocked on the door and scattered love all over the sheets. That was what had happened, and each of them dealt with it in their own way, *is this what they call "love"?* Bella had asked in her clumsy English, but Mads hadn't answered, he'd just nestled closer to her and tempted her with the same old *you're my baby*. He stroked her bottom, so quietly, so calmly, with the whole palm of his hand, *baby*. Bella froze and he looked at her, *should I stop?* But Bella's mouth was totally dry, she didn't have a single word left in there, she shook her head, it was crystal clear, God's presence was strong, *my baby*, Bella couldn't make a single sound.

Everyone sees the world from their own position and Bella's position was on all fours. She had nothing to hold on to, but her knees held her up for a long while at a time, he would leave her suspended there for a split second as he studied her body and she hung there longingly like the scent of someone's perfume in an empty room. Just as poetic, just as awkward. She painstakingly moved her hips into his hands, and like a praying angel he kneeled on the mattress and spilled what he had across her back. Bella wanted him as close as possible, she could hear his heart beating its lonely beats deep inside him. Half asleep, half awake. The nights flowed along, soaked into her skin, all the way up to her ears, right into her eyes, closer and closer with each passing day, them being this close made it hard to breathe. Someone had found her at last and now she lay curled up in a quiet corner of the world. In those big arms where no one could see her, where no one could hurt her, where oblivion almost swallowed her whole. It was so quiet she almost forgot herself and her vast gluttony. It was no wonder she'd stood with her mouth open from the start. But Bella knew what safety was like, knew it inside and out, it was claustrophobic and suffocating, she felt it always. Every time she took a breath she breathed in air that had passed through his lungs, air that had made his heart beat, it was absolutely impossible, she was breathing the same air that made his brain work, it was too stifling. Every morning she listened to his breath drying behind his tongue. The sunlight got tangled in her hair and she studied his stubble, the light stung her eyes, she felt her thoughts trying to escape from where they lay buried in skin, dozing and floating in Mads's arms. She had to just lie here without making a single sound, without moving a muscle, for as long as it lasted. She had to feel all the good, keep away all the bad. She had to just try to be anything but herself, totally calm in the quietest corner of the world.

Mads blinked and looked at her with a drowsy, sparkling look. *My little sugar, who are you?* He ran his hand through her hair, put a finger to the worried frown between her eyebrows as if to push it back in, *I love you*, he whispered, and before she could answer he stuck his tongue so deep into her mouth that it rushed into the most inaccessible places. There was something about his face, the way it moved when he stood in front of the mirror and washed himself, like he was a complete stranger to himself, like something was slipping through his face that he had no control over. The air was clammy and stuck to her lungs. Mads met her gaze in the mirror and smiled, *did you know that? That I love you?* Chills ran through her, she couldn't answer, couldn't say anything. She stared at his face in the mirror, which smile should she look at? Which image was more real? How could he not get scared seeing himself? The sun was rising, leaving a yellow veil draped across his bare back; wet light filled the room, filled the whole mirror, and all she wanted was to have him inside her. She looked at the silly grin smiling back at her from the wall but it showed nothing, not fear, not cold, and not God's plan or whatever it was that made him just keep coming closer and closer.

Mads loved Bella, and Bella tried to love Mads. There was something about the overwhelming feeling of just that: love leaning against her body every day, her hands glowing pure purple. All the overwhelming things in a person's life. Bella had the ability to love, it wasn't that, she loved Nellie, but Nellie sat there lit up by her expensive dresses, surrounded and loved by her own children. There wasn't enough love for everyone, Bella almost didn't dare feel it but something had wedged itself in between them, it wasn't the same as before. She had tried for a long time to tell Nellie that there was nothing wrong with her, but Nellie just sat there, surrounded by children's laughter, and looked at her condescendingly and thought she knew everything. Nellie obviously needed help with the children, quite a lot of help, she could barely take care of them all, and now that Bella had moved in with Mads they could maybe take little Olga at least, just for a little while, so that Nellie could keep her head above water? But Nellie had harshly refused, almost gotten angry. Bella started to cry. The refusal was a slap in the face, sister to sister, what was anything worth if she couldn't have even this? A flood of tears surged all the way up to her face, pushing ahead at full force. Right out the whites of her eyes, Bella felt it all with perfect clarity, her eyes were bulging out of her head. Bella stood there with her chasm and her arms, harder and harder, *please*. The sun shone bright, the light slipped in and out among the leaves and made everything so quiet, the eternal fluttering of the butterflies, everything was so fragile, so thin. Bella begged, on her knees, but her tears were real, her skeleton hands were radiant, Nellie had said no, had basically spat on her.

69

Bella didn't know what to say. She looked at Nellie, who was frantically trying to be nice now and lighten the mood, *so let's just sit down and have a bite to eat, then?* Nellie said, but Bella's mood was all used up and enough was enough. She had spent the whole morning with Olga picking flowers for Nellie, but now she didn't know if she even wanted to give them to Nellie, because they wouldn't make her happy. At least not when she saw the trampled flowerbeds, Bella understood that much. Because Nellie could grasp none of what Bella was trying to give her. She didn't know what love was. Bella felt it inside her, everything just getting harder and harder, the darkness in her eyes flashed out when Nellie came over with a handkerchief to try to wipe away her tears. Bella stared through the window and quickly wiped her own cheeks. She saw the butterflies, God's purest creatures, among all that green—Nellie couldn't even grasp that, the greatness of creation, all the gifts God had given them. Bella stared at it all, she stared at the eye on the butterfly's wing looking back at her. That ardent eye resting on her. The picked bouquet waiting in a vase on the dining table. Her throat was warm, making it even harder to breathe. But Nellie said nothing else, Olga had been with Bella all day, the wind had died down, the leaves had reached up toward the sky. The sun had been big and yellow, glowing right on Olga's cheeks. Olga had beamed and come running over with one flower after another. Red little cheeks amid all that green. It had taken so long to gather a whole bouquet, and Olga was surprised again every time the root came loose with a big jolt and half her arm got black with soil, but Bella had waited patiently for each and every flower and Olga had laughed every time. The laughter had made Bella go soft, all the way down to her bones, and then and there Olga had felt completely hers, standing barefoot in the middle of the flowerbed, squealing happily. Time almost stood still, an eternal moment then and there, while the bouquet grew and grew. Olga had torn up all the flowerbeds in the garden and Bella could still hear her laughter, it made life easier for her, easier for everyone. But now, in the living room with Nellie, it was like the laughter had been torn out of her breast. Bella pulled the chair out from the table, sat down, raised a spoonful of potato soup to her mouth. Her eyes were dark when she turned her gaze to Nellie. Nellie stared back. Something had gotten wedged in. They were smaller now than they'd ever been, circling around each other, far apart, like two frightened animals. Bella felt it run down her cheek. *I've made a hole here*, she told Nellie and took her hand and Nellie felt straight through to Bella's heart, felt the warm area under Bella's face, her skin was too soft, *God won't forgive me*, Bella whispered, but Nellie's eyes just turned blank and she started clearing the table.

After that day Bella refused to talk to Nellie. Everything had hardened. That was the end of the teas and dinners, the moments of closeness. Bella was done. It glowed on the

71

walls like a coldness of its own, enough was enough, and on the last day she stood in the middle of the living room and tried to say goodbye, she tried to bring out Olga's soft, warm laugh, but she no longer knew how something could come out soft and easy and all by itself. She picked Olga up and looked around while holding the little child's body tight against her chest. Everything was shining from within, so shiny and hard wrapped around each other, but this was the end. Those two dark eyes, she had seen with perfect clarity how Olga had the same sudden chasm inside her as she herself did, the same precipice, the same deep shadow over her heart. How everything crashed down inside her. Bella felt what was in there working its way out, and it came out, but it came faster than Bella had imagined it would, Olga opened up and turned inside out and there was no way to close her back up again. Bella tried everything she could, hugging her a little tighter, trying to distract her. But it was too late, Olga wriggled out of her grip with a fury that knew no bounds, the force coiled around her little body. Bella pushed Olga's little head back down onto her shoulder, and rocked her back and forth, around and around, but Olga didn't calm down like she used to. Her red face got redder and redder, one lurching movement, body against body, layers of seconds, flashes, strength unforgiving and holding on so hard it hurt. The more she tightened her grip the more she felt it; round and round and round she rocked her little red child in her arms. She looked at the flowers in the green vase, saw where the light followed the lines of hand-blown glass and rested on the petals and filled up the flowers' little heads. She looked into the dining room where everything lay in darkness, almost like a funeral, it was so depressing, all the dead things in there. Bella's gaze was crystal clear but Olga refused to be quiet and obedient, she strained as hard as she could and then fell to the floor with a little thud. The astonishment made Olga pause for a few seconds and stare at Bella in shock. Like she was saying straight out, *how could you?* Bella looked at her little niece and her feelings left her body, she turned ice-cold. The two-second pause lasted an eternity before Olga brought out what lay deepest inside her, before her tongue came into view and harsh howls found their way out of her little mouth. Olga kicked the table leg and the vase tipped over and fell to the floor. Bella stood staring at her, at the broken vase and the water running in little tracks that made dark stains in the carpet. There was so much noise in that little body, Bella really couldn't bear it. She looked at that fiery red scream, the big mouth, what could Olga have been through that was really worth screaming for? It was like she was getting her howls from some truly awful place, Bella couldn't stand it anymore, and she left her there on the carpet, screaming like mad, in a ring of tulips. There was nothing more to say. Bella walked out the door and didn't look back, there was nothing left after this.

THE LAKES OVERFLOW WITH WHAT FILLS THE HEART

B ELLA HAD STARTED to realize that she was respon-
sible for no one but herself. There was no such thing
as unconditional love. Everything had demands and limits,
everything had shapes that would burst and crack, even
Nellie had a thousand conditions Bella couldn't live up to
and even Olga had gone from leaning softly against her chest
to staring into her face in horror. Bella turned to God, went
searching through everything written in the Bible, there in
black and white, the unchanging truth. But something had
gone deep, Nellie had left her, she really had taken sides. Bella
had asked only for Nellie's love but Nellie had rejected her
the first chance she got and now Bella was just waiting for
everything else to be taken away, for the invisible betrayal,
for Mads's real face. Bella burrowed further under the covers
and felt the future lying there beside her, outstretched and
warm, it flickered and cleared up in turn, the white covers
lay there like big piles of old snow, the echo didn't fade, it

ran along the walls, ice-cold, there truly wasn't enough love for everyone, and reverberating inside her: *what kind of person are you?*

There was no way out of this, no way back. Bella stood on the lawn outside Mads's house and watched the sun melt over the fields, everything seemed so endless. The kingdom of God extended so far out across it, all thin and fragile at the edges, the holy creation, was it really worth anything? The lakes gleamed like enormous jewels and covered her eyes with a sweaty blur, her cigarette glowed between her fingers, she took a long drag. The cold in her chest, the warmth on her lips, she heard Mads coming home, she heard his movements, every step made the floorboards creak. The birds chirped louder the darker it got, the insects seduced each other, he walked over and put his arms around her and something sank inside her, *I want you to remember this when you're alone*, he whispered, and the hairs stood up on her arms, *I want you to know I'll always be here for you*. The vibrations settled into the grass, all the resistance inside her that could let go but wouldn't. The dusk filled her pupils as more and more stars came out, everything sparkled straight into her soul, big and dark blue, the sky above the porch, the light between the trees, *I'm not going anywhere*, he repeated in her ear. Bella had to blink to understand it, the rocking chair and the creaking when Mads sat down in it, the large mouth, the rocking and the hands and the skin over his knuckles. To enter someone's life with a new grip, a handshake, a hug, a hand on the thigh, it was a test of strength. To shine straight into someone's heart—that was what Mads had done. He had gone straight into the darkness there. She couldn't quite grasp it, this huge beam of light, how do you open up to a stranger? How hard do you push yourself, how tight do you grip the hand reaching out to you? Bella had to blink to understand it, the smile in the mirror, the real face, the ice-cold trickle in her blood, *who are you really?* Mads pushed her hair behind her ear and kissed her, she couldn't think. He dazzled everything, and the light went into her. Mads wasn't going anywhere, he shone right through everything. She felt his warm hands on her body, she was transparent, completely exposed.

Mads held on tight and didn't let go. His recurring desire didn't end, it filled her from eye to eye while the crickets shrieked louder and louder. The noise clung to the house walls, everything shifted in small waves, muscles rocked her back and forth and lifted her almost weightlessly into his shining arms, flies buzzed and butted into the windowpane. *Baby, baby*, she felt the voice coming from his diaphragm, what exactly was he trying to say? He put his hand on her cheek, *my baby*. She looked at him and felt the warm hand, *was this a game?* He was so gentle, so careful. There are no coincidences. Her eyes welled up and she tilted her head back to let the tears slip back inside. He peered into her with the tender look he'd first given her when she had opened up a little, halfway, a crack, it was like the light had wormed into her brain and forced its way out from within, these white membranes covered her whole field of vision, the starlight, the crying, she tried to blink. Memories pooled behind her like a white soup, they sloshed every time she moved her head, the pure death by drowning. Trees rustled, distant and powerful, the kingdom of the lakes, the eternal wetness pushing ahead, it all was out there working its way toward the center, like it wanted to rush at her. The series of events, everything with Nellie and Olga, had an insistent force, she saw traces of mold along the foundation of the house, black branches reaching up the wall. The damp potato cellar, the smell of earth, the cold wet fingers, the thin nerves in the skin, the sensitivity around his eyelids. The half-open mouth against the floorboards, the dampness and the light. Everything was in motion. Two obliterating shapes right on the basement floor, two bodies completely alone in the world, constantly trickling, dazzling in through the window and into her mouth. Mads just repeated what he'd been saying all along, *baby, my little sugar cube, I'm not going anywhere.*

But church discipline threatened from the congregation, they were living in sin, something had to be done, and Mads turned around and proposed to Bella with a ring that melted around her finger the second he put it on. The summer had rubbed off on her skin and her golden color glowed against the brand-new gold. Bella got a new white dress, she ran her fingers over the seams, the thin threads along the bottom fold, she felt how easy it had been and how hard it was going to be, the sewn-in silk threads, it was so beautiful all by itself. Bella stared out into the world, everything just got tighter and tighter but no one could see how tight, how the dress pressed its rough seams into her skin, how it left a red band on her waist that dug deeper and deeper, but Bella stood, uncomfortable, the way she always had, and forced a little smile into every stinging movement. The dress was obviously too small, it dug in where it shouldn't and made her skin flare up as she carefully swayed from side to side. The big folds of the wedding dress spread out so light and easy and the world was reflected in her ring. She took a few careful steps forward, in front of the mirror, the folds were so shiny, the fabric spread out like a large bright flower whose petals calmly accompanied every movement. Bella and Mads had come together in faith in God and now they were to be united in the name of our Lord Jesus Christ.

The flowers, the trees, and the tolling of the church bells hovered in the light around them, as if gasping for air; the sweet dark smell of her perfume followed her like a strange shadow, the sunlight fell between tree trunks in floating columns, the whole churchyard lit up. Mads ran his hands over the bright freckles along her forearm. Everything crowded so close together and the horizon line floated sharp in the distance. A blue landscape of veins lay spread across Bella's wrists. She looked at her husband, everything felt so soft and shapeless. They sat in front of the rose bushes in the sunset, each with a sky of their own in their eyes. Bella leaned in, toward the marriage in the middle and the church in the background. Her low laugh blended with the cream from the wedding cake Mads had bought. It would be easy, it would be the two of them. Her lipstick extended slightly past her lips and Mads wiped it from the corners of her mouth and kissed her, hard, as if once and for all. The wide flowerbeds and long lines of gravestones, the living and the dead surrounding each other, it was unbearable, a gasp moving through the air, the earth packed tighter under them, Bella was taking part in the deepest thing there was, she saw right into the story. She tensed every muscle in her body, she was terrified. The silver threads buckled inside the soft fabric, the burning red ribbon, she felt it with perfect clarity, it ran through her like the dull thud of falling trees, *I mustn't cry.* Her eyes were so hard, like shiny marbles, *Lord, stay close.*

It was as if the happiest moment of Bella's life contained the most horrible moment too. She couldn't quite grasp it but it hung above her, perfectly clear, as if the trees were holding their branches in a very particular way just to mock her. The world was a whole, she could see it, but it was like she was standing just outside it and there was nothing she could do but cry. No one let her in. She undressed slowly, hung her wedding dress on a hanger and hooked it onto the door frame, she stood for a while in front of the mirror, slowness in her body, all the little moments of closeness, she reached her arms as far back as she could until her shoulder blades touched like wings. Bella fiddled with her ring, half-naked in the dark, pulling it off and putting it on like a child's game, married/not married, married/not married, until the ring finally slipped out of her hand and rolled under the bed. She lay flat on the cold floor and looked, and she saw the ring, its engraved looping cursive writing, everything she had to promise to have and to hold, his body in exchange for hers, a promise before God, his forever. She lay with her cheek on the floor. Finally, a peaceful moment for Bella—her body cooled down, everything was quiet. She stayed lying there looking around, everything felt so crystal clear. She saw her dress, it had given her everything she wanted, that white angel up near the ceiling with smears of light green at the bottom of the skirt; she looked at the bridal bouquet with the red poppies, on the bedspread; everything inviting her in, all the colors, nature really had rubbed off on everything. Bella felt the quiver in her tailbone, there was something down there at the bottom that no one really wanted. She looked at the ring glowing in the darkness, God's burning promise right on the cold bedroom floor. The ring carried what it was meant to carry, she was Mads's now. She heard him moving around down in the living room and she stood up slowly, draped her dressing gown over her shoulders. Everything went so slowly. She heard the wall clock and the new fire that had just begun to crackle downstairs. The dressing gown trailed down the stairs after her, pale pink, she could bear it, she had to, she saw Mads so clearly every step she took. This was the most beautiful thing in the world, all she had to do was accept it. And like an empress she floated silently into the living room, the ring sparkling by itself upstairs under the bed. She found Mads sitting by the fireplace, his corpse-white skin in front of the flames' flowing light, Bella didn't understand that Mads wasn't seeing what she saw. She stood before him in her pale-pink train, a broken flame of her own.

Mads ran his hands along her body, she was soft as butter and her throat was dry. The dressing gown was stained and the belt that was supposed to close it hung down at the side, frayed, her breasts were visible, *Bella, my wife.* He wanted something from her but there was no way she could give it to him. They had given each other hand and name and let the gold flow into its mold. She was married now, the ceremony was over, but the flames were voracious, always ready for more. She stared at the fire, everything that got so hot it changed color. The house really shone that night and existence roared inside her. Blinded by the light, Bella collapsed onto the sheets, and a towering pillar of fire and hell rose up all around her.

The die had been cast, and this was how the marriage woke up the day after its birth and in all the weeks and months that followed, it was like something had turned around in the open door and the spaces were filled with everything she didn't want to see. The grain in the wood, the twig holes in the wall paneling, the cracks in the windowpane, the eternal grin in the mirror, everything she hadn't noticed until now. She had promised before the altar that she would obey her husband in good times and bad, stay with him until death did them part. She had promised it all in every moment and every silence. Even when she was washing herself, even when everything got dirty, she had promised him everything; when sorrows settled under her nails and she washed herself as often as she could—even then. In the bathroom, two strands of hair had stuck to the wall, two dark straight hairs. She found them next to the bathtub. One short, one long. Waste matter from two people who'd been naked together. She plucked one strand from the wall and laid it against her skin, covering it with her hand. She opened her hand and it was still there, his dark little trash. Everything that had left his body. The same way he was going to leave her.

AUSTIN, ILLINOIS, 1886–1900

T HE BLINDING LIGHT fell through the window, it fell
through everything, it raised dust and flies, it raised so
much that Bella felt sick, it overflowed everything, and in the
middle of the overgrown marshes and dammed canals, in
the middle of arms and legs, in the eyes in the middle of her
face, Bella lost it. Nature really had rubbed off on everything
and one day the walls just cracked, the light sliced right
through everything and she saw it turn real, a kerosene tank
must have overturned and the fluttering in her pupils was
just the flames pouring out of the windows and, even though
they were surrounded by this watery landscape, destruction
had obviously taken hold of her and their house burned to
the ground. The blinding light fell through the ruins, it fell
through everything, help had come too late and they had to
just stand there, hand in hand, watching everything burn to
the ground. It was horrible, nothing could be more horrible
than this. Their house was a freshly smoking ruin, oozing with

water, and Bella felt the cold spreading between her shoulder blades, everything that had been so hot that it changed color, all of it, it had to have something to do with strength, she saw her bones through her skin, this was too symbolic for it not to have consequences later. The water that had put out the fire mixed with her tears and finally Mads found them a house with the insurance money from the old one. They had to bear it, they had to hold on, put one foot in front of the other, but Bella felt it glow in her hand, she felt the warning on her skin, something much worse was going to happen.

In the new house they opened their arms, they had promised each other that something new and bigger would emerge from this disaster, that God was just testing them, getting them ready for something greater. So Mads and Bella stood there with open arms, they stood there and accepted the impossible, the abandoned, everything that didn't stand a chance. They accepted it and raised it up into the light and kissed it, these newborns who had skin and hair and were nothing short of the start of everything, these little orphan children no one wanted. It was God's beauty. Bella understood now, in this moment, that this was what she had come into the world for, it was obvious. She was ready, Mads fetched them and carried them in over the threshold, let the light into their eyes and let them eat straight from the table. There was no one who could save them except Mads and Bella, that's what they said, that Mads and Bella were made to do it. As though appointed by God. If Bella couldn't give birth to children of her own, she could at least open her door to these little angels. The why of life and the how of life gouged both of her arms, deeply, she prayed to God, when would he give her one of her own? She looked down at the little bundle in her lap, *this is all I have*. She looked down at her dirty fingernails—the dirt had burrowed deep, she caressed the first little child's cheek, trying to keep the little one pure, *this is really all I have*.

Bella lit up every time a new child came into their home. Bella in her worn-out dressing gown, with arms open wide and hair tangled from sleep, with a face so soft you could slide right into it, all she could give, all she could hold. She opened the door and took them in, stroked their hair so softly and breathed in their smell, hugged them tight, kissed their heads. She trembled, there was no resistance, the little bodies slid right in, *people should always give away the best thing they have*, Mads told Bella as a smoldering red autumn sky lay over the trees and the raw air filled their lungs, *and now they've given their best to us*. She scrubbed them clean and put them under her dressing gown, right next to her chest, she held them so tight, terrified that something might happen to them. She protected them as long as she could. Mads was right there, standing in the doorway and studying his little family on the mattress, *it's like they're carved out of your face*.

The years went by and there was always someone who needed new parents, the light fell in dusty drifts between the trees and the lakes, toward the great void ahead, and the children were opening their mouths the whole time as if they didn't understand what family they had wandered into. A gentle touch slipped past, the big gasp; destruction had clearly not released its grasp and the children turned pale so fast, for no reason at all. She lay them right up against her to give them her warmth, but they never accepted it. Was that why? Was it the destruction that ran in her blood and crept out and took them from her? Was that it? She took the children to the doctor but they just disappeared into themselves and no doctor or nurse could ever bring them back out. Bella looked at Mads with tears in her eyes, there had to be something, something about her in particular, that made her so much worse than everyone else, because it inexplicably happened every time, *I can't get close to them anymore.* She wasn't a real mother, they didn't want her, it was like they realized that. Everything lay so heavy upon her eyes, the children died no matter how many times she prayed or went to church and got them baptized, she stood there with death in her arms and nothing slipped free. She felt it down to the bone, she was gray, short of breath, retreating into herself. Just like them, blank and lifeless. Mads was obviously using her as a mirror, she saw the shame shine in his eyes, why didn't he say anything? She kept the children safe as long as she could, but she couldn't recreate how everything used to be, she felt his gaze on her body and felt sick, the yellow and sickly light, but Mads just came closer, ran a hand over her forehead, and whispered, *my little sugar, I'll always be with you*. But Bella knew it wasn't true. Mads took her hand and Bella gripped his as hard as she could. The wet light wrapped around them as they stood face to face in the middle of the living room. Black branches of mold crept up the foundation wall, nothing had ever happened in this exact order before, but now it did, she felt it on her body, a sequence that snuck out and blocked every doorway.

Autumn was coming. Pitch-black darkness slithered down from the mountains. They had put the three little ones who hadn't crossed over to the other side in the same bed. *This might be the last mild evening we'll get*, Mads said as the twilight streamed down his pale face. There was surrender in his voice, as if the poignant tone between them was gone forever. There was silence there on the porch and something inside her fell to the ground, *if God wills it*, she whispered against his forehead and kissed him. Here it was, abandonment, impossibility, the silent scream coming out of them, Bella was filled with it, oozing, it was almost sickening. Mads repeated after Bella, *if God wills it*. Bella kept her loved ones safe as long as she could, she had held on tight, but this was a test of strength. Bella went inside to check on the kids, make sure that the last three lying in bed were still breathing;

she looked at them from the doorway, *who's going to love you if I don't?* The sleeping bodies lay there so motionless, she went over to them and put her lips to their foreheads, they squirmed and she smelled the sour milk, she just had to sit perfectly quiet and hope they would still be breathing in the morning.

Bella wondered for a long time what his last memory of her must have been. What he thought about her, how something must have twitched in those suddenly deep eyes, how his face must have looked when his heart stopped pumping more blood to the rest of his body. Was he scared? Was he thinking of her when he fell? Was the grass soft? Bella could only imagine. It was an image she tried a hundred times to work through. Mads beneath the heavy green branches in the yard, a memory she had never had. Mads with his suntanned face, broad smile, the burning mirror in his eyes, just a sad fantasy. Mads was playing in the yard with the children and a few hours later he was dead, that's what the neighbors said. The autopsy report said: "He died of an enlarged heart." And Mads really did die on a summer's day in 1900, July 30th to be precise, whether from an enlarged heart or a cerebral hemorrhage wasn't easy to tell. But it had jolted Bella so hard when she walked through the gate and saw all the neighbors standing in a circle on the lawn. The muffled scream stopped in her throat, *Mads!* but nothing found its way out, and they'd put a blanket over him and now they were standing there looking back and forth between her shocked face and the pale face on the ground. Bella's brain was staring into itself, she saw Mads from afar and she saw his face right up close, his features, there was something stiff over his mouth, *Mads, my dearest angel*, her voice was so thin it almost cracked. The words slipped from her left ear into her brain's right hemisphere and out the ear on the other side and melted into thin air, moments of nothingness, *my beloved baby, my little sugar cube.* Her brain knelt down and kissed her insides, mouth to mouth, farther and farther in, but the gaping hole had closed and now she was left with nothing but silence between her hands. Bella went from room to room, she couldn't find her way back, nothing was where it should be, the only thing left of him now were his clothes and the semen stains on the sheets. She lay down on the mattress. The suffocating taste in her mouth. The spots formed a broken pattern around her, he had died in the yard and not in her arms, Bella couldn't breathe, who was he really thinking about in those last seconds?

The doctors who performed the post-mortem examination said that everything was normal. Life had taken its course and sometimes a person just dies. That's the way it is. Everything given to someone can also be taken away, that was what had happened, and now his smell lingered in the air like a wound. A life was gone as quickly as it had come. Everything was murky and uncertain. She was wearing the same clothes she'd put on that same morning, *please*, she whispered, choking with tears. Bella had to blink to understand it: Mads was gone, gone forever, he wasn't there anymore. The disaster had finally announced its coming and now it lay side by side against the whole of existence. His life had simply disappeared from the face of the earth.

Bella had never imagined that Mads would be the one to disappear; three little girls had survived, by the grace of God, but Mads had to be sacrificed so that Jennie and Lucy and Myrtle could live. His hand had been so cold and the cold had crept up into her face, her brain—she had tried to warm his hand, but then she had to let go. God's will was stronger than hers, and for something to live something else had to die, and Mads had been lying there with his cheek on the ground, lifeless, under the trees with the taste of dirt in his mouth. The taste of vomit was dammed up with her tears, the story spun around and just got longer and longer, the girls blinked and grew bigger and taller with every passing second. They had come to her like little gifts in white dresses, silk ribbons in their hair, it had all been so beautiful and impossible, and now the dresses were too small and Mads was dead and Mads's brother suddenly got it into his head that there was nothing natural about enlarged hearts or bleeding brains or playing in the yard. Someone here was out to hurt and destroy. Bella sat there with the three little survivors, with all that sat unsolved in her heart, how could anyone explain what had happened? To a furious older brother who wore his grief on his sleeve? Why was this strange person coming into her house? Oscar Sørensen came straight into her living room and looked at the flaming words winding across the wall: *The Lord our God is a consuming fire.* Bella went over to him, *it's from Scripture,* she whispered, *I embroidered it,* she whispered. *But that's not from Scripture,* Oscar said harshly. He didn't like her, that was obvious. Bella put a hand on his shoulder and felt with perfect clarity that everything she said would be used against her later, *I mustn't cry,* she whispered to herself before she fell silent inside her tight dress. She looked at her brother-in-law, *what do you know about love, Oscar?* Her voice was a rustle of cigarettes and port, Bella looked Oscar right in the eye, she could be as belligerent as him, but she held back as much as she could. Oscar stood there big and smooth as steel, just like his brother, hot-tempered, merciless, with flushed cheeks. Mads had been in the earth for a whole little eternity, why would he come up with this now?

The alcohol had burned away all the softness in Bella, she didn't care anymore, she had nothing left to give, she sighed, *you don't know a thing about your brother or me.* She looked at him, everything clenched so hard over her belly and tightening around her ribs, the red band glowing even now, this inflamed depraved life, everything pushing in, compressing her. She held his gaze as she got undressed. All the sympathy bouquets, there were so many—the smell was sickening, the

94

petals in circles around the vases like dead butterflies' wings. Yellow pollen mixed with the dust in the air, all scratching her lungs, it was so hard to breathe. Oscar with his tragic nature, with his zealous moral body, as if it had less desire than anyone else's. It was so quiet there, standing face to face. Bella in milk-white panties in front of the red sofa, bearing her whole self, filled to the brim with grief and fury, Bella stood there stripped down, there was nothing else to take off, nothing else to put on. She was a woman against a red background, the widow's ritual, naked in the middle of the living room in front of her brother-in-law, it took a great many tears to accept it, *get dressed*, he said. Bella raised her hands in front of her face. It was so dark in there between her hands and her eyes, she saw the girls playing out in the yard, the gray roses in the vase, the noiseless flames in the fireplace, she lowered her hands, *you don't need to worry about me, Oscar.* She put her arms around his legs and squeezed tight, but Oscar Sørensen tore himself free. Bella had to hum a little to herself before she stood up and slipped a nightgown on. She was totally dizzy, she saw the flowers' shadows on the wall, the light falling, the prayers sticking inside her palms, the wedding ring on the dresser in the hallway. Oscar obviously had more to say, *who are you really?* Bella had to smile, he was just like Mads, she saw the resemblance around his mouth, the desire from deep inside, what was foolproof in every man. He stared at her, everything vibrated, a pool of sin, she reached for his hand but he pulled away, Bella looked at him for a long time, she was a widow with three miracle children, what did he really think?

Oscar had stormed out the gate, furious. Bella felt it, the proud moment had stiffened in her chest. She looked all around her. The flower water was still brown, the faint smell of rot filled the room, taste of dirt in her mouth, smell of mold and damp filling the house, carpet drowsy and soft beneath her feet. Jennie, Lucy, and Myrtle, the immortal little angels, followed her up the stairs with tiny steps, little mincing dresses—shining little proofs of God's implacability but Bella couldn't give up, she had to keep going. She owed it to them and to Mads, she had to keep them alive and she held them as tight as she could until her arms hurt.

Oscar wanted to dig Mads up, skull and bones, skin and hair, everything would come to light. Oscar wanted to see it all with his own eyes, he wanted to see his brother's body, see what she had done to him, this despicable chicanery. So they dug Mads up, put his legs and arms on the table, Bella's tears continued to flow, Oscar Sørensen's grief was so shameful, it was vile and vindictive, but he refused to pay for what a full autopsy would cost and Bella rejected the accusation, she wasn't going to pay a penny for that man there, so the legs had to go back into the ground and the examination ended with no results, Bella collected Mads's life insurance, but rumors had spread, voices scratched in her ears, she couldn't take it, the preposterous neighbors and their prune-brown eyes.

Bella put her bare feet on the cold bathroom floor. Everything welled up inside her again, Mads's warm kiss on her spine, the little glowing points, the infinitely warm skin, she felt her stomach muscles tighten. She missed Mads with every cell in her body, down to the last fingertip. She let the water run over her shoulders and plucked a hair off the bathroom wall, he wasn't all gone. She sank all the way into the tub until the water filled her so intensely that she thought her time had come, it filled her mouth and nose. That deep love he'd been so sure of. The longing for death in every single moment.

Bella collected the vases and emptied the flower water into a bucket, splashing the brown water over her fingers; she dried herself on her apron and divided the newspaper between the girls sitting wide-eyed. The girls were so careful in everything they did, they placed the flowers onto the newspaper one by one, in a row, reaching precisely to the edge of the table. Bella's hands were shaking, she had to get outside, get some air, and only when she was a good ways from the house did she turn around and take a breath, but her hands were still shaking. The strong scent of flowers hit her in the face when she returned. The girls were standing in the hall, in front of the mahogany sideboard, almost completely still in the afternoon shadows. Everything was so different, so quiet. Bella squinted in their direction in the half-dark and her insides clenched. The big flowers hung heavily down over their vivid eyes, *what are you doing?* Bella shivered. But the girls didn't answer, they just stared at her expectantly, each with a wreath in her hair. The whole thing was so overblown she couldn't stand it. It was like they'd just carelessly picked some random flowers from the roadside. How could they do this to her? Bella shuddered, they had braided death into a wreath and put themselves in its center, eyes clawing for new details, those pink nostrils with their almost invisible movements, the breath in their small bodies, the smell and the dust pushing in on her. All that symbolism grabbing onto her face. It was suffocating. This wasn't about them. Mads was dead, the man who had carried them home and given them names, who had let them breathe against his chest. She looked at the gray flowers. It was a clear sign. She saw it with perfect clarity—they were heading straight toward a shining death.

FISH TRAP LAKE,
LOWER LAKE,
CLEAR LAKE,
LILY LAKE,
STONE LAKE,
AND PINE LAKE

LA PORTE, 1901

NOTHING WAS POINTING in the right direction, she had been given this whole life but what was she going to do with it? Bella acted blindly. She put an ad in the *Chicago Tribune*, maybe she could trade the house for a farm and get away, she couldn't stay here anymore. There was no mercy in any of this. At its purest and most naked, even when kneeling against the pew—nothing. Bella had to get away, from this congregation, from the rumors, from everything breathing down her neck, and in the end everything worked out, she was offered a deal for an old pig farm a little ways outside the city, in La Porte.

Bella loaded everything onto the wagon; she had sewn the insurance money into the lining of the little coats and hidden their valuables so that highway robbers wouldn't find them. Then they left—Myrtle, Lucy, Jennie, and Bella. There was nothing keeping them in Austin, it's a free country. They took the cart road past the church and the graveyard, past all the white crosses stuck into the ground, so dearly loved, so dearly missed. The church shone in her burning eyes, a mother always knows a longing from the depths but Bella wasn't a mother, or a wife, or even a sister or a daughter. She was just a grieving widow on American soil.

Bella raised her daughters to have faith in God, faith in the good in people, at least that's what she said when someone asked, when the new priest poked his head in. *You must get down on your knees*, she might say, *so God can forgive you.* Her faith was so strong, so clear. Fortunately, the neighbors and the congregation were just glad to have a respectable person come to town at last, a Christian woman. Mother of small children. Widow with three girls. Bella took a deep breath, felt the never-ending faint prickling on her face—love with its grotesque red formations had gone too far and now she lay in a new bed in a big house like a crater of flowing hair. She said her prayers, closed her eyes. Bright sunlight streamed through the thin curtains, revealing the hint of a vaguely wondering smile in the corners of her mouth, everything swung so fast from one wall to the other, flickering one second and clearing up the next. Everything was there already, Bella had acquired two hundred acres of land with henhouses and stables, the cock's twisted shrieks and the horses' sweaty bodies. It was impossible to stand still. Nine lakes surrounded the farm, lakes that sparkled in the sun, still and clear like wet midpoints between the forest and the prairie. The pigs rolled in the mud, Bella felt her heart in her chest, everything pushed ahead, it was entirely natural, everything was ready and waiting for a new start.

Bella tried to tidy up. She hung her dresses in the closet—expensive, splendid garments with soft skirts, countless corsets—Mads had bought them all for her, the fabrics were so smooth, the girls loved to hide in them and trail the grand trains like queens. Their bare feet against the wood floor made a fat, sticky sound and Bella felt relieved in the presence of this new life. Hair flowed in waves down the little girls' backs, it was the most beautiful thing Bella could think of, the soft baby hair, the golden fabric, all so soft and so fragile. She saw the leather boots shining in the hall, the worn, freshly oiled leather, the gloves he had given her. Everything felt so violent. Laces could be pressed so close to her eyes, caressing her smooth skin, touching her thighs and hips. This grief was so simple and stupid, that was exactly it—the drapery of the dresses, the beauty, all the nice things that only got nicer because he was dead and grief goes looking for meaning, there was no way to get an overview, everything was so trite, and the dresses still made her cry in great violent heaves.

The rooms in the new house were painted the muted colors of ice cream: vanilla, raspberry, pistachio. Everything was supposed to be new and nice, but everything wasn't new and nice, nothing would ever be new and nice. Anxious restlessness filled all the rooms. Bella had spent a lot of money so that the children could each get their own room, large rooms, lots of space. There was room for everything, for the most fragile movement, the grossest lie. Bella staggered around in heavy leather boots trying to do everything herself; she gathered her skirt in one hand and eggs for the basket with the other; the sun painted the muddy edge of her skirt, shone through the thin linen apron, through all the brown. Bella really did everything herself, she shoveled manure and milked cows, she stood in all the dirty, mean things, but she couldn't get through everything in time, and the storms came and took the roof off the pig house and destroyed everything she had tried so hard to do. She washed her hands every night, but the sinful shadows wouldn't go away. There really was something about Bella's face, it was like a single big muscle was gnawing its way out into the light. As if something had rubbed off on her, as if the animals' movements had done something to her, as if working with pigs and calves had forced something new out of her, as if the new farm boy who suddenly appeared out of nowhere had something to do with it, it had to be something. The change was obvious, and Bella saw the birds come flying in over what they called Fish Trap Lake, screaming, plunging into the water for insects. She felt the frightened eyes of the birds on her body, eyes mapping out every single threat, every movement, eyes always ready, it was like she was looking straight into herself.

Bella smiled at her daughters over dinner, deep red and affectionate beyond all bounds, maybe hope existed after all, they were staring at her with their urine-colored eyes, Bella really wished she could protect them and keep them hidden away from whatever was coming to destroy them, from this world, this stepmotherly gaze of hers, the insatiable depravity waiting around the next corner. She closed her eyes. She felt it from the depths: temptation and sin would come onto the scene.

Bella woke up every single day with a face that didn't know any better and stared with a look of disbelief at her three non-biological children. The only survivors. Curious little things with cheekbones and lips belonging to someone else. These little strangers who grew too big, who endured her, three little roaming witnesses with eyes that soaked up everything they saw, she hated them almost. Bella kissed her cross; the light fell along the back of her neck, along the gold chain around her throat. Everything lay so thick around her eyes, her daughters, big and soft, undulating like waves, they really could bear too much of her love, much too much. At night Bella would stand in the doorway and just look at them, something she had done ever since they were little—she had to just watch over them, make sure they were still breathing, but she saw how something ice-cold had taken up position in their legs, shivers and twitches pointing inward, while an icy coldness emanated from the walls. The shivers shot through their little bodies, this silence in the house, the obvious threat, she saw so clearly how her dreams and nightmares had rubbed off on them. This constant resistance all the time, this invisible in the visible—everything was revealed in them, blood, tears, urine, together in the same bed, their legs tensing in their sleep and kicking her in the stomach. It was repeated every night, red blood vessels in their eyes, insane strength. They just clung tighter to her body and dug their fingers deeper into her stomach. The whole time confronting her, *God, if you still see, can't you take them away?* They weren't hers, when were they going to understand that?

Her lips burned, her mouth was dry, there was nothing simple and easy in either faith or life, she had to withhold, keep her balance always. If only she could have closed her eyes and prayed in the old way, but her childhood faith was no longer where it used to be. She couldn't tell them the truth, the whole simple truth. Who did they think she was? They could braid her long hair as gently and sweetly as they wanted but they'd never be a part of her. She could kiss their heads and melt into them a little, but never all the way, never completely. She didn't believe in them, not for a second. All her saliva was gone, she felt their warm bodies next to her. *Down on your knees*, she said every day, *down on your knees*. And they went down on their knees and said their prayers. The hair stood up on her arms, she pulled them close, she longed so intensely for a sliver of truth. God was leaning upon the house, weighing down with all his might, Bella could feel it. She had to be strong in her faith, she was being pressed down into the mattress. Her brain tried to raise her up with the power of thought but her body was parked, the tousled little heads sought her gaze, everything prickling on the front of her eyes. Something broke off and cracked open, but it wasn't God. The little tongues of fire glowed down in the darkness under the blanket. The endlessly warm skin, something in their eyes that refused to give up.

Bella sat with the knot of muscle in her chest, with the scream and the bruise, and there really had been something about that farm boy who came by, Ray Lamphere. He came just like that, on his own two feet, as if the substance he was made of had never hardened in the mold, as if everything about him just continued to flow no matter what he said or did. She'd seen such things before, discomfort in sunken eyes utterly untouched and broken at the same time. Even his hands, Bella felt sick all over, the lack of control, and Ray Lamphere leaned his face right into hers, he didn't look away, and she studied him for a long time before she agreed to anything. He got a cup of coffee and stuttered a bit before getting to the point, he was just wondering if there was anything she needed help with, even the saddest man in the world needed money, and Bella had to take what she could get, even in the gray light and the thunderstorm, even if it was covered with dirt and obviously criminal. She looked

107

at his slumped shoulders and smelled booze on his breath. There was just something about the way he wore everything right in the middle of his face, this vagueness, it was almost provocative. Ray Lamphere stood there with his big furrowed hands and a cautious smile while Bella quickly glanced at the ceiling, *Lord, stay with me.* This had to be what mercy looked like. Motherly softness. It was pointless to believe anything else. She showed him into the barn, to the attic room where he could put his things and stretch his legs. The golden wave from the cornfield lit up his face, his dark eyelashes reached out in a wild and beautiful arc, Bella didn't understand why this made her so happy but it flowed through her like liquid gold that whole day.

IF YOU TELL SOMEONE A SECRET IT'S NOT A SECRET ANYMORE

CHICAGO, 1893

GRIEF WAS INCURABLE, it changed everything forever, but how accurate could memory really be? Her memories, all her loving thoughts, lingered inside her, right there in the middle, but what really happened to the love between living people while they were still alive, when they were in the same room? Could they really nurture it? Did it lay in her arms as strong and beautiful as she remembered it? Did the move east change how she looked back, change what she could see after so long? What was it that shone through the cracks, that hurt the pupils of her eyes? Something had happened before Ray Lamphere knocked on the door, long before Mads's death, long before Bella had set foot on the pig farm in La Porte. Something had happened that would lead to something else and make everything even more unbearable. It must have involved a lie, or was it just one of those times Mads had said she could do what she wanted, he couldn't take it anymore, and so she just did what he said, just did what she wanted. She had to, she couldn't stand this idiocy, this secret hidden demand. So Bella left. She went back to where Nellie had put an end to their sisterhood. Bella went back to Chicago, to the opening of the World's Fair. There was something almost magical about it, those reconstructions of good old Europe. Something swollen and hard, right in the eye. The big bombastic World's Fair was right in front of her, they had built a whole continent out of thin walls, houses, roofs and windows. A luminous Europe with a melting smile and ice cream in every corner. Bella slowly floated down the streets, balanced on her tiptoes, saw it so clearly: a reflection of everything that could have been itself but was too flimsy to be. An impossible dream. The World's Fair with its forty-six participating countries, the White City where buildings rose up out of the blue. It was plaster and marble, everything was so thin and hollow, domes and arches and it was all going to just be pulled down as soon as the Expo was over. A flimsy dream that could break apart at any moment, just a little kick and her foot would go right through the walls. Bella looked around, at the green patches of lawn and the squealing children on the Ferris wheel. It all had to be reassembled across the Atlantic, no wonder the Norwegians were disillusioned. A small orchestra had squeezed into one of the cabins and it played while the wheel went round and round. Everything so adrift, so afloat all together, everything just thrown into the air and it was pure chance what you ended up with when it came down—round and round, only thin seams holding it all together, this powerless European dream. A false memory. She felt shivers running up her arms. Little howls were hurled from swollen red mouths up in the air. Everything rose and fell with the turns of the wheel; all the settlers stood looking at everything they'd left behind. Everything they had in common and everything they should write home about. The simplicity of the monumental. The craving in the belly. The dream that surpassed reality. Every morning they had to realize the same thing—that their imagination wasn't up to the level of reality. They had to try, through deep alcoholic sleep, again and again, to believe that they had made the right decision; it took strength to endure oneself, especially when everything around them was collapsing. The World's Fair was supposed to bring hope. With its weight and its visions. But Bella just stood there while everything flowed into her eyes. It flowed and flowed. She had always wanted to get to the end of the world but it turned out the ends of the earth weren't far enough, had never been far enough, she felt the taste of something stale and chunky in her mouth, the sharp taste of devilry. The coals glowed beneath the grill and the smell of charring meat oozed down the streets leaving a thin layer of grease along the window frames. All the children were so happy, but no one could recognize themselves in any of this. Everything she had wanted to leave behind. Bella

113

saw the shimmering light in their eyes, she was surrounded by equals but that brought her no relief at all.

Bella walked past a lottery booth, stood staring at the prize list for a long time before buying a ticket. She was hoping for a better future, for her daughters, for herself and Mads, she hoped with all she had that something would change, that her little family could finally have a little luck, that God could provide for a little more future-oriented hope, that she might not fear Him so much now that the children had proven resilient enough to evade death. Hot and pale, she studied the prizes. A pram and twelve free eggs, a piece of ham, there was nothing she either needed or wanted. Bella tore open the paper and waited for her numbers to be called out. She just wanted to walk away a winner, was that too much to ask? But Bella wasn't a winner, and Mads's green eyes pierced through the thin buildings, stung between her shoulder blades. Everything imitating reality had become too thin, she saw from a long way off how the future shot out in an arc and then twisted back down in her chest, everything was made of the same stuff and the dreams lingered under her eyelids, dark, burnt, right on the grill. Bella couldn't save anything, no one called her number. She felt everything inside her burst and seep out, Mads's eyes running like luminous veins through her body as if he was watching her every movement, her every thought, Bella saw exactly what was happening here at the lottery booth. She fused with her destiny, the truth finally shone through the cracks, everything fell flat, it was so clear, she was forever and always a loser, she couldn't win anything, her skeleton was falling apart, she didn't get even one single ham. It was perfectly obvious, the future had abandoned her the first chance it got.

The Fair was swarming with people holding meat and bread in their hands. Napkins, ketchup, everything unfolded before her eyes, this really was the new world and she was entangled in it, everything crept and crawled around her, she saw it all with such clarity, it lay so thin in her lungs, flickering around everything she owned, everything attached to her body, her soft skin, gloves and hat and dress and coat, the thin layer of fat smearing itself onto every surface. She stared straight into America, into another reality—the great possibilities, the wet dream everyone was talking about. Bella found the Thams Pavilion, which might tell her something about where she came from. There towered Old Norway with its woodwork stinking of tar, with dragon heads, pointy spires, it was dizzying, the thirteenth century rising straight up from the ground, tongues of flame pointing straight up at the sky. It made sense in its way. Something tightened and suddenly it was like her body was hanging together a little more firmly and steadily than before, like her arms and legs no longer felt like someone else's or loose in their joints, like her eye had finally found its way out of the labyrinth. Bella had chosen to leave Norway, of her own free will, she had

done it, but now she stood here and felt everything she'd
left behind. Everything was connected with everything, in
Selbu, in Austin. Everything that was inside her had been
on its way somewhere else for so long. Mads was sitting back
home in their house and Bella was standing in the middle
of Chicago in this new thin city and seeing how the sunlight
passed straight through the thin roofs lying slanted in the sun.
That big tower at the top of the Pavilion. Who was she really,
when all was said and done? The blood trickled inside her,
melting, deadly. It was aglow, it burned into her bones, pale
pink, bread and meat, there was no resistance anywhere. As
if this big building was about to fall on her at any moment.
Everything Bella wanted passed through her mouth and her
eyes, she couldn't hide it, everything she desired was so visible on her face, a big glowing chasm, straight in it went, she
was standing in the middle of the world without anything to
hold on to. Bella chewed slowly, people laughed, sang, took
out their fiddles, every imaginable language piled on top
of each other in a low, swirling hum that filled every nook
and cranny while children chased each other and skidded
through the gravel. A place opened up a little way ahead,
as the melody and the light settled like a white skin around
the heads and pale faces flowing along in dancing polskas,
roundels, springars and gangars, and amid all the meat
and music and dancing, amid all this softness and warmth
undulating and swimming back and forth, amid new-mown

grass and sweaty dark locks, she saw him. Sunbeams flooded in through narrow streets. The future didn't exist, the past didn't exist, everything was perfect. Bella owed no one a thing, she was free. The stave church had plunged into her chest, impaled her, and opened up a new space inside her. Everything loosened, liquefied, everything she'd had to bear for so long trickled out into her fingertips, ice-cold. She saw him over there, took a few steps, the light outlined his hat and his jaw, she saw it in his neck muscles, the curly hair by his collar, he was one of them, surrounded by his own hard edges, she could recognize a soft-spoken Scandinavian when she saw one. The harsh taste of fat swelled in her throat, her pulse pounded in her temples, he stood in the middle of the street staring at her, Bella felt it, this man was everything Mads wasn't and couldn't be, the clarity of his gaze, the independence of his movements, it was now or never. It didn't matter how she was going to remember any of this, sons and daughters of Norway raced past her, everything was going so fast, she stood there totally rigid and felt the light trickling through the cracks, she tried to resist but she saw him come over and the blinding light fell.

It was Peder Gunness standing there while the sun glowed sinking down behind the church spire and the evening light melted down over both of their faces. Bella's heart lay open, bruised and alone, floating in free fall. *This is just a feeling, it's like everything else.* She hurried off in the opposite direction but felt his gaze crawling up her whole spine and suddenly felt his hand on her shoulder, she felt him encircling her as if he'd understood that she, her whole self, was an invitation, some leftover scraps he could gorge on. She saw in his face something that appeared and disappeared again, like a wave of something she shouldn't defy, without her noticing it the clouds had gathered into a dark shadow in the middle of the sky. Bella shivered with eyes fluttering, two half-open lips. Her spine had burst into flame, and right then and there the pain in her body was so intense that when the sky opened and rain poured down there was no doubt about it, she was standing in front of Peder Gunness, soaking wet, she could feel it, something was spreading all the way into her bones.

The sky was dark and heavy, it stuck to her lungs. Big raindrops fell from the sky so slowly and his gaze had dropped into her cleavage. Thick, wet moments fell from the sky and she couldn't move. She saw the wedding ring on his finger, this was impossible, she couldn't stand here anymore, but Peder Gunness's hands were so big and Mads flowed out into her blind spot and her dress stuck to her ribs. Everything was so close to her skin and at the same time so far away. Her guilty conscience disappeared as quickly as it had come, and she should have realized it even then, when Peder Gunness came up behind her and took hold of her, first with one hand, then the other. She should have understood it when the resistance started to leave her body, when he put his coat over her shoulders and pulled her to him, she should have understood it when her mind left her body and everything went blank, Mads couldn't survive this.

Peder Gunness had kissed Bella in the rain where everyone could see. Under the big crowns of the trees. The smell of caramel and hamburgers had followed them all the way into the bedroom, they were all alone in the house, he had peeled her wet dress off her and the screaming inside her had stopped. Peder subdued everything inside her and his kissing mouth was absolutely enormous, it couldn't happen any other way. Bella left all his red caresses exactly where she wanted them, exactly where the skin was thinnest, where the change was most evident, there was no doubt in any of their movements. But time and grief lay there like two broken legs. They were both married, their bodies belonged to other people, and yet Mads had no place in this. Peder saw the landscape of blood playing out in her wrists, the thin blue rivers, it was so visible in her face, everything swelling in her, spilling out in big thick streams. There was no doubt about it, she had come with the northern light, there was nowhere else but here, the moment had been created, and Peder was wading through her with soft creamy movements in the pale Chicago light. Everything was so purposeful, aimed so right that both of them gasped for breath, the big gasp slid through them both like a mirror image, he knew exactly what she wanted, how she wanted it, and when to take it. When he finally reached her child-ish little mouth he just wanted to drown in her, pull her in with him, watch her let go, swallow, and disappear down into the darkness.

It lay so powerfully on her eyes. Bella felt his beard against her cheek, his harsh breathing, his lips tearing and struggling. Peder was a bit like Mads, he sought comfort in the same way, but his hands were so obvious and hard and he didn't let her get away for a second. He pulled her head back until her neck couldn't be stretched anymore and her dark hair flowed over her shoulders, the boundlessness of his movements, so eager, so hard, the red caress, she couldn't say no. But everything has a beginning and an end and when she woke up the next morning she saw him so clearly. Something inside him had emptied and not been refilled. And now he lay there with his naked body, asking for too much. Moments of closeness. Why did he have to stare so pleadingly, like a little child needing to hear that he hadn't done anything wrong. Human softness always needed to be taken so seriously, it was ridiculous, Bella couldn't comfort or forgive him for anything, he had to take responsibility for himself. He brushed her hair away from her face, his whole body so pleading. He tried to kiss her but she pushed him away and put his arms back on his body, *we shouldn't have done this.* She got dressed and moved toward the door,

Peder followed her down the stairs. The thin seams holding everything together were coming apart, it had to stop at this. Bella didn't turn around, she had to go back home to Mads and the children. She hurried down the stairs, through the yard, out the gate. She felt Peder's longing gaze on her back but he didn't say anything, he didn't even shout. Peder Gunness thought that that was the end of things between himself and Bella Sørensen, but the end would turn out to be much worse.

HOW DO YOU HOLD ON TIGHT TO SOMETHING ABOUT TO BREAK?

BELLA WAS LEFT ALONE, and with what? A small inheritance and three little creatures breathing down her neck while Mads lay rotting in the ground. It gurgled faintly somewhere inside her, a hundred invisible beats, all the way in, to the last memory in the back, the one she had peeled off. There was just a hole left, a black hole she could fill with whatever she wanted. She rubbed her eyes and yawned in a single long breath. The girls ate breakfast at the big table, the light twisted into something dazzlingly beautiful between the cutlery and their tongues, between teeth and metal, between leftover porridge and slabs of butter, down into the opening in the dark. The craving in her belly didn't go away. Ray and the other farm workers had already been out in the fields for hours. Bella scoured the porridge pot, her cross gleaming weakly on her chest; she looked out at Clear Lake, where the water lilies were blooming on the surface of the water, they dove so quietly with their smooth brown stalks, roots going all the way down to the bottom of the lake, getting tangled in the underwater plants and dividing the sun's rays between them, all the way down. Glistening green and muddy, a great streak of light. The lake glittered and the sunlight poured in onto the kitchen floor, Bella reached for her face, it always opened wide, a golden glistening membrane, she felt it with her whole self. The ravenous roar in her chest. Bella scrubbed as hard as she could, she looked at the little bodies stuffing their big greedy mouths, what was she really supposed to give them? There would come a day when they couldn't have any more. There would come a day when the porridge wouldn't be enough, a day when she would have to say: Stop. She wiped the kettle, the damp lay over the property like a faint mist, she tasted blood in her mouth and looked into the deepest depths and saw it so clearly. She stroked the girls' hair, her hands were ice-cold, she felt it with her whole body, how everything slipped in and out of its place, *if God wills it*. There was something about thoughts and words, how they got paralyzed, how she remembered things or didn't, the burning waist of the wedding dress, the inscribed ring, how thin silver threads could cover over a crazy wound and an awkward memory. How could anything have been the way it was without her remembering it? She thought about everything that had happened, the tremendous lack of details. The smell of the dishwater had pulled Mads right back into her body. All their actions had piled up on each other, heaving death up into the daylight and dragging the roots from the other side with it, making it hard for her to grasp what had really happened. The thin brown slime, the impossibility of forgiveness, Bella felt it, she felt everything with her eyes, the why of life and the how of life, the groundwater seeping up between the floorboards. Ray Lamphere stared her almost to death, every day since she'd let him in and given him work, anything that was given to her could be taken away but Ray just gave and gave, the little lambs he midwifed, yellow with amniotic fluid, moments of closeness, his fists stroking the udder and bringing the newborn lamb to its mother, the most fragile of the fragile, traces of blood everywhere, it was unbearable.

Everything could rip apart—her face was too open, she felt it with her fingers; everything that had to be stored up and counted and done the right way. Bella felt she didn't belong here in this gigantic landscape of Germans and Finns and Dutch, idiotic Norwegians, and yet this tremendous lack of detail. God's merciless power. The hay that had to be dried, the milk that had to be churned. Pork scalded and salted and sold. Lastly, intestines had to be stuffed. Bella was surrounded by equals, blood, tears, urine, flickering so quietly, noiselessly, the grieving wives who'd been on the same ship as her, the families who lived and died for each other, yet she didn't recognize herself in any of them, there was no rehearsed and practiced love in them, no hint of routine. She felt the quiet rocking, waves passing through her chest, her iliac crest grinding against her pelvic joint. She had dragged her body after her, as far as she could, to the ends of the earth. The longest movement every single time, all the little steps, one foot in front of the other, what was shining through the cracks? She counted her money every single night, sorting the expenses into one envelope, the income into another. She carefully jammed both envelopes between books on the bookshelf. Bella felt the hopelessness, felt it in every shrieking bird, in their great soaring flights across the sky. Bella counted and counted, she saved what she had left over, the girls would get nice shirts and the workers new work clothes, she had a plan, it was so simple, and yet she felt so guilty, she had really dragged herself through her childhood and youth but still didn't know what being her should feel like.

The trees dropped their branches, threatened to break and fall on top of them, she felt the grace on her body every time the storm gathered strength and the birds screamed in the treetops. No one could withstand this. The wind chased the house, beat against the walls. She had to ask Ray or one of the others to cut the branches down, the trunk was swaying too much. The girls stood at her side, barefoot, freshly washed, as the clouds gathered silently around the house. The girls' little fists clutched her wool skirt, the powers rolled in across the plains, the gate slammed shut down by the road, *Lord, let your light shine upon us*, Bella looked down at her daughters and her hands looked so big compared to theirs, she felt the nausea at the back of her throat, the great streak of light, how far could she go without breaking them? Big and small falling in and out of place, all the little lambs and piglets, the little bodies that would only grow and grow, her hand that would just get smaller and smaller in theirs until the skin on her knuckles was just a transparent little baby bird. Bella stared at the big oak tree, saw into the depths with perfect clarity, the tree was leaning in closer, the trunk could snap any minute, she wasn't ready to be crushed under the weight of a fickle God, *do you hear that wind?* The girls nodded and darted into the dining room, the sky changed color. Bella really tried but it hurt so much to look at them, all their endless fear, it was so stupid, muscles clenching under the skin, veins bulging out, *God sees you in there too.* Bella tried to fight off the nightmares, she really tried, she watched over them all through the night, she kept a vigil. She kept the strangers out, staring at the bedroom door, *well here we are, at the end of the world*, she stroked their hair. She saw the clenched fists, the breath coming out between half-opened lips. She couldn't protect them much longer, she could clearly see how they were trying to hide in her arms, all the things they did for her forgiveness, all the things Bella did with the sky. The house creaked as the wind roared and tore at the walls. The girls were so defenseless under her gaze, yet they loved her with all their hearts.

129

BELLE

BELLA HAD BEEN GIVEN this whole life but there was something about the order of things, how Ray kept getting closer. Often right up to her cheek. Suddenly. With his voice much too deep into her ear and his hand at the very bottom of her hips. She really should have kept her distance, but there was something about how he always kept close, especially when the children were at school. A lurking shadow all the time, right there in the falling light, she saw it, there was something about the way the curtains moved gently by the window frame, right there, as if the wind was hinting with just its little finger that there was something there, that he was there, pointing with its finger at everything going on, watching what Bella was doing. But Bella stood completely still, in speechlessness, she saw everything that was inviting itself in. That was how it must have been, totally speechless, the churchyard with the shining light, all the people who had been given this earth, had been loved so deeply and buried so deeply too, the great silence. Bella could only imagine what it must have been like, in the deepest depths, how the wind must have forced its way in from the window and made a crack, how Peder Gunness must have realized it before he actually realized it, how he must have heard his own lungs murmur. Totally speechless. She saw it so clearly, how Peder and his wife must have lain there next to each other as the sun seeped in through thin curtains, light falling on her lifeless body. She who should just wake up normally and kiss her husband and lean against him with all the warmth she had in her body. The world's easiest movement. The warmth should spread as it did every morning between two people who loved each other. The open window let in a little shiver, Peder must have seen it, the little opening, how death crept in, he must have lain there and peeked at her just to be sure and then taken her hand, just to do something, to feel the actual cold while she lay there pale, stretched out in her nightgown, as if he was trying to understand what had happened. Maybe she was already blue, or yellow, or a little stiff around the lips. Bella saw it with perfect clarity, the icy cold that could fill a body right up in just a few seconds. From one second to the next. There must have been something almost peaceful about it. The little puff of wind from the realm of the dead, the twitch in the corner of her mouth, the lightning that could fill a whole human face, the intensity in her eyes, everything completely gone. Mrs Gunness must have been all alone in her own world, enclosed, done with life. Being abandoned by your loved ones too soon—that was a detail that didn't go away, neither with a funeral nor with crying. Bella knew all about it, how grief settled into the body and changed a person forever. The clenched knot of muscle in the chest, the scream, the bruise. Bella shuddered. The silence and the church bells, their droning sounds tolling through the city. Clouds and trees, horses and shops, everything resting so quietly. Everyone stood there with faces turned to the ground and felt the crumbs of soil dig into their eyes. The short time from when death arrived to when Mads was to be lowered into the earth, it was like an eternity, so cold, so damp, the open grave slowly filled up again. Three spadefuls of wet dirt. Sweat ran down her back, had someone really made sure that Mads wasn't breathing before they put him in the coffin? Peder must have stood there all alone and thought exactly the same thing—a little patch of death could slip in anywhere.

There was so much grief a person had to put up with, maybe that was another reason why Bella went looking for Ray more and more. It took strength to endure herself but also everyone else, and she saw something in him, he asked for so little and incited so much. She filled the kettle, a bird swooped in over the faraway mountains that were like a blue ice castle in the distance, she rolled up her sleeves and went into the bathroom with the kettle of boiling water, filled the wash basin, and watched the steam rise. Bella saw it in the mirror, it was as if something new had opened up in her face without her realizing it. She saw it in her mouth, in the frown that used to press down between her eyes—it was gone. Instead there was something expectant there, something that could no longer be hidden, *guide me, Lord*, Bella was almost frightened by her own uncomfortable expression, the big smooth muscle in her face, *I can't find my way on my own*. She slapped her mouth. *Guide me*. Harder and harder as her mouth got redder and redder, like a soft little hell getting closer and closer.

Between the first and the second time Bella saw Peder, she had lost everything and he had become a widower. Maybe that was why Bella's face shone with a haze of desire veiling her eyes as she tried to beat the shame back into her body, but a new landscape really had opened up and Peder really had packed his things as fast as he could. He'd hitched the cart to the horse, tightened the girdle under its belly, and brought with him his two daughters and everything he owned.

Peder Gunness came to La Porte, to pear-shaped Clear Lake, to the big farm with its soft colors and endless fields and a hundred and fifty pigs. Her heart sparkled and heat melted into liquid with every touch. The world had given a sudden jolt and smoothed out her worried frown lines as if everything really had happened for a reason, as if she no longer found herself in the pool of sin, the little puff of wind

in the curtain, the shadow on the window sill, the little butterfly, Ray had come around the corner and suddenly Peder
was there on the front steps drowning out everything inside
her as he'd done from the beginning. Wet mist lay thin and
sticky over her eyes and Peder's lips had been swollen from
the first second he saw her. This really was a new landscape,
and a time of miracles, the summer flooded in through the
window almost too much and all of a sudden Peder had given
Bella his late wife's wedding ring, everyone bore their own
grief and now she bore his. This was the cycle of forgiveness,
it was perfectly natural, it was how people were linked to one
another. Bella took what she could get, she took everything,
she could certainly wear a dead woman's gold.

Her new freedom was not as self-evident as she'd thought
at first but she continued anyway. There was food that had to
be sold before it rotted, sick carcasses that had to be buried
as soon as possible, but Peder really had brought with him
everything he owned and luckily she could keep going the
same as before. She dipped a comb in a bowl of water and ran
it through her hair, it almost disappeared, those tiny seconds
that separated one action from another. There was something about the simple movements, the short strokes, fingers
against scalp, from one moment to the next, the long strands
of hair being drawn to their full length in her hand. From
all the way in to all the way out. Bella sat before the mirror
with a pale mouth, full of saliva, she no longer knew what

made up the greatest part of her life, the memories or the lies. The face in the mirror, which image should she believe in? Bella had to clutch the dressing table until everything hard and uncontrollable disappeared back into her soft hair. Her eyebrows were just trying to be normal but she wore a face that was trying to conceal the most fragile thing in a person's life. She patiently shaped the thick braid into a soft crown on the middle of her head. Most of the decisions had been made long before Bella knew it herself, the only thing she could do was concentrate, stay the course, and brush her hair away from her face. The shape of her head got so soft when she put up her hair like that. Maybe another life really was possible? The world had jolted once more and she had a whole family now, she was newly married, suddenly rich, she was part of the story of creation. The new world. Hairpin in hand and another in her mouth while the cross dangled beneath her chin, with her red lips and white skin, she saw it so, so clearly. The demand for justice lay shining there behind both her eyes, in her whole face, like a frozen movement, it pressed up against her in the mirror like a brutal prophecy. Everything given to her could also be taken away, she knew that, she truly bore the punishment for every shameful thought. Bella heard footsteps coming up the stairs, why couldn't Ray Lamphere just leave her alone? Bella kissed the cross, met her own gaze in the mirror, flinched when she saw its smile, and there was a creak outside the door, *please*, *guide me Lord*, she whispered as he came toward her, but Ray didn't answer as he pushed her to the floor.

Bella Sørensen had become Belle Gunness. And for a little while her farm in La Porte was a place in the world where everything rose up higher and higher, the walls almost ripping themselves out of the ground and all the colors trickling out of their cracks and spreading across the sky like a soft silk ribbon, making everything one hundred percent permeable and alive. Belle admired her ring in the sunlight—in less than a year they'd gotten married. Strangers could believe whatever they wanted but it was like she and Peder had been together forever. The ring was simply where it had always been, where there'd been another ring before it. The ring was supposed to be there, the strict promise between man and woman, between the spouses and God, she was going to keep all her promises, she was going to keep her back straight and her head held high like any respectable woman. Belle couldn't take her eyes off her ring, the gold Peder had given her, it was so symbolic, he had even written her into his will, it was all or nothing, it was honorable, powerful, the words came out so quietly, one after the other in the right order, he said it like it was a well-kept secret, like it was in spite of and not because of, and she had to suppress a grimace when it came, *I love you*.

Everything had a beginning and an end and for now everything was ready and waiting in the middle. But there was something about the vastness of the sky above her and the number of colors it managed to cast across her property at once, over the delicate lace hung on the string to dry, the girls' faces and Ray's shifty eyes, God seemed so close, in every movement, in the animals and birds, as if he was pressing down on her on purpose. The quiet, menacing worries every single day out here, she saw exactly what was happening, it made the hairs on her arms stand up. Peder was always sitting in the living room, always a burden in the living room, she carried the laundry up to the house, she could just work, she didn't have to think, she put the tub of dry clothes on the bed. This was the biggest thing, but also the hardest part, she didn't even know if it was fair, was her life supposed to look like this now? Should she be grateful to her husband? Belle's hands were shaking so much as she folded her undergarments, *Lord, have mercy on me.* The lifeless tongue filled her with intense sorrow, *this is how the world is.*

Peder was in his chair reading when she came down to the living room. She stopped and hesitated on the bottom step before walking over to him and kneeling down. This isn't going to work. He pulled her between his legs and kissed away what was left of the worry on her lower lip. Belle stared at him as she brought his hand to her chest, *feel here.* Her heart was pounding like that of a terrified animal, wounded and trembling, galloping straight into the barbed wire fence. Tears ran down her cheeks. He felt with his hand where she'd asked him to. He looked at her, worried, *Belle, what's wrong?* But the skin stuck to her brain and there were no thoughts left in her head, she sank down in front of the fireplace and stared into the flames. The fire licked at the logs, a flickering settled into her pupils. The small distance in there between the shadows, there was something there, in that blue point, the quietest moment, a simple muscle memory. Her hand slowly changed color. The silence and the flames burned fast. The warmest fleeting thing, she couldn't catch it. Belle was floating all alone, Peder called out to her but she'd disappeared into herself, she felt the barbs against her heart, the flaming spine, the rusty thorns. Everything that was punctured, everything that was out of control, the eternal blue hours, it flowed and flowed and when Belle finally pulled her hand back it was blistered, oozing, wet. The skin pulled back before it opened up completely, Peder screamed but she didn't hear, she only felt insistent hands on her body, he understood so little, there was nothing new about this. She lay with her cheek against the carpet, she looked at her hand, the skin had unfolded and the burn was glowing in the middle, she just wanted to know where the line was.

DESTRUCTION IN AN OPEN FACE

NOTHING STAYED PERFECTLY STILL. It never had and it never would, and Peder and Belle were in the last stage of capitulation. They had really fused together, among the pigs and the goats, but the smile on the wall had gotten distorted and Belle had turned her eyes to the sky. She filled the basket with wood and left the fire burning through the night, wandering sleepless from room to room, barefoot, in her nightgown. She put log after log on the fire and made sure everyone was warm and stayed alive. The candles bowed softly in their candlesticks, like pleading, surrendering bodies, soft and abandoned under God's gaze. Things kept building up. Belle couldn't help but push Peder away, it was obvious that something was drawing to a close. There was no doubt about it, she knew he could feel the huge bird wings flapping through his chest, the shadows in their eyes. She saw it in him, the wing beat passing through him, the thing that fell through everything. It was like something had melted and rotted away by itself. Peder was completely defenseless, he was standing at the edge of the cliff. There was something about his eyes and how his shoulders had been pointing in a different direction for so long. He had done it all by himself, he had built up that distance with his own two hands. Always facing away from where she was in the room, always somewhere else when she walked in across the threshold and stopped in the hallway. She felt the small vibrations when she lay in his arms, his hands' indecision along her hips. She looked at him from the bed where she was unfolding, seconds of lingering, dry lips, hands that didn't move as fast as before, and he didn't sink into her, he blinked and was obviously lost in something else. Belle knew it, he was never going to finish, she recognized cowardice and powerlessness when she saw it. She couldn't feel like that, she couldn't have this doubt so close to the edge of her face. She needed someone who loved her with his whole heart, someone who meant it. Who'd fight for it, who'd leave marks on her body. Time forced itself ahead and the moment came all by itself, the light had pushed through the cracks, she'd seen it so clearly, the little brown butterfly in the window, the dying movement at the edge of the world. The small gesture of something big. The meat grinder had been too close to the edge of the shelf and Peder had fallen, and so had the meat grinder, and now he was lying there all alone as his life trickled out onto the floor. The grinder made a gash and Belle was left standing there with the great silence inside her, looking at the open head. Her breast rose and fell but something inside had collapsed and she thought about how she'd lain so open for so long. As if everything had been in its most beautiful order, as if they'd had never-ending parts in the middle to feed on, *like a moth to the flame*, on its way to the same destruction. She'd lain naked, so many nights in a row with her nightgown pulled far up above her navel, her crotch completely open and hairy and straight out into the room and Peder had protected her openness. He had. But he'd also had a good supply of it, this openness that kicked itself right into her face, that worked toward a grand finale every single time.

Belle's ring sparkled on the dresser. Everything flashed and trembled inside her. The burn on the palm of her hand and her numb heart tried to outglow each other. Everything had to kick itself free. She followed him upstairs. Washed him, kissed him. It was her marriage lying upstairs calling out for her. It was her husband. Her nearest and dearest. Her biggest and heaviest. Always all the way deep down. Creaking. Silence. The calm, she couldn't explain it. She pictured his charming smile, the one he had fallen asleep with, the one with congealed blood on it, the one she had seen the first time they met. Everything had rubbed off on everything and the rainbow floated toward her in shining colors. There was lightning in her. The kissing mouth, the flickering sensation when he opened it, his long red tongue, his body always wanting to move into hers. Peder had been so boundless in the way he tried to protect her, in the way he had given her his daughters. The girls, the wedding ring, the burn, everything that kept her attached to this world. How much would she have to take before she could take anything back? She went upstairs and looked at him but there was nothing to say. This was how it was. A thud, then it cracked. He had gotten the bowl of brine all over him too, what a sad fate. This was the last red caress.

Peder lay motionless on the sofa while the doctor examined him. He looked like he was sleeping. The skin on his face was already a little yellow, ice-cold, permanently sealed, turned inwards. His chin had stiffened and his mouth had slipped open, even in death he couldn't shut his mouth. The blood glistened in a thin streak running down his face, Peder always expected that when he woke up everything would be the same as it was before but he wouldn't come through this time, there was just no more light left for the two of them. She saw it so clearly, he had left, he was gone for good. The dirt had gotten too far under his nails one day and now there was no going back, she felt the taste of mud welling up in her mouth. The dim light of afternoon sank into the room and Belle put her lips to his cheek and felt his beard scratch her, *I just wanted us to be close*. His smell was fading. It was so simple, so quiet. A story had come to an end, and at last a new one could begin.

LA PORTE COUNTY POLICE:
FIRST INTERROGATION,
MRS. GUNNESS, 1902

– Can you tell us what happened?

– He was sitting in the kitchen next to the stove and he bent down to pick up one of his shoes, and he bumped into the stove and the meat grinder and bowl of hot brine fell on his head. It totally knocked him out, so I put vaseline on the wound and told him to lie on the sofa and rest. As he lay there, he called my name, for several hours, and then at some point he disappeared into himself.

– Disappeared into himself?

– Yes, he was gone from me, he lost consciousness. He didn't hear me.

– Was he a nice man?

– He was a very nice man. I wouldn't have married him if I didn't think he was nice, because I wanted a kind man, not only a kind husband for me but a kind father for my children. I never heard him say a bad word the whole time he was with us.

– Were the two of you happily married?

– As far as I know.

– Was he kind to your children?

– Yes, kind to me and kind to the children.

– Do you suspect anything, are you afraid someone might have come in and hit him over the head with the meat grinder and killed him?

– I have never been afraid in my life.

**REALITY IS
LIKE DEATH,
IT CATCHES UP
WITH EVERYONE
EVENTUALLY**

BELLE WORE HER CROSS in the hollow of her throat as clearly as she could and said her prayers and did everything the pastor said. She had rubbed away the tears and the blood with the palm of her hand, and now here she was with five children who needed food and clothes and a father figure. No one gave Belle Gunness anything extra, she had a family, she had a farm, she had expenses and debts and was more in the red than in the black but everyone thought they knew better, everyone thought they knew the truth about what was going on out there on the Gunness farm. There were rumors that she hadn't been good to Peder, that she was involved in shady business. But no one could know, because no one had seen, her love—how her nails dug into his skin, how she held him tight with both hands, how she felt every little muscle contraction. They hadn't seen her when she put the girls to bed and the whole avalanche just tumbled onto her and turned her eyes totally transparent.

They hadn't seen the child's skin, smooth as butter, they hadn't seen what she sank into every night, irresistible, what cut her in half and filled her with heavenly hymns, what was so soft it held her prisoner, the tousled hair, the smiling eyes. Belle loved it all so much she wanted to break it. No one had seen any of that.

Belle hung out the sheets and the handkerchiefs to dry in the wind, little white peace flags. But soon she had to defend herself and her daughters, they had endured much too much of this flood of rumors, for much too long. She saw the clarity and beauty of their large pupils, little black points of eternity with endless questions. They didn't look like her at all, and certainly not like Peder, they didn't have the same freckles and moles, they didn't have the same unpredictable features above their mouths. Their eyes were too big for their faces, as if they could never have their fill. Greedy bottomless pits. Belle looked closely at the little bright heads, anyway she couldn't take responsibility for everything Peder left behind. So she sent his daughters to the nearest family, light seeped in between the cracks, she couldn't have that responsibility, she didn't know them, she looked at them before she left them on the cart, a fluttering in their pupils, what was moving in there, how deep did their love really reach?

Belle held her nearest and dearest close, the only thing she wanted was to throw herself into her own daughters' arms and comfort them. Belle saw how they'd secretly started copying her, how they made little fists every morning and every night. Their prayers imitating hers, knees on the floor, neck bent, hands under chin. How they got ready in front of the mirror and scratched their lips until they were fiery red. Belle shuddered, were they making fun of her? She saw how detailed it was. The simple in the monumental, they lay on the floor with their hands above their heads and prayed for their lives. It glowed from their fingertips. But it was as if the girls knew it too, they knew that they were the ones pushing the scream out of her, Belle stood there with the northern light tangled around her ribs, the children's red cheeks, she watched over them with the darkest love, loved them with every fiber of her body, but the plunge inside her was deadly, they had to pray, there was no way out. It was a difficult love to bear.

The whole plan had been a lie, everything that was meant to be, the rich man's sweat and the waves in the water, the sons of Norway and the men from Buskerud, it was not what God had willed, it came from her and her alone. It hurt to love, and Bella had not been entirely honest with herself. Not with Mads or with Peder either; she was never honest with anyone. Belle had spread her love as carefully as she could, giving what she could without losing herself. She saw it in the mirror, the sin that swallowed everything with its dark smile shone capriciously back at her, what had failed and been forsaken pushed up in her face. Her jaw cracked, so hard, *what kind of person are you?* She drew breath into her lungs and felt it almost explode. It was their fault, they had let her decide. They had begged. Reality caught up with everyone eventually but no one seemed to notice, the farm boys just continued to work as though nothing had happened. They whipped the cows in from the blizzard as they always did, even though Peder was dead and there was almost no money left. Belle had lived for so many years with intensity and power in her hands, with the little shadow under her chin, should everyone just pretend that everything was the same now? She couldn't keep her balance, she had tried but ultimately all there was to see was the end, nothing else. It had been inevitable. Ice-cold endurance threatened to destroy everything she had.

The snowflakes landed in her eyes like icy white flowers, everything she didn't want to remember, everything she'd genuinely forgotten. The world seemed so empty. The snow melted away toward the tips of her eyes, this farm had been and remained a power center of nothing, a beautiful doom. She found herself in the middle of a drunken dream, lost in a white horizon, *Lord, guide me,* she felt pressure on her chest, the congregation's expectations, the freezing cold that stuck to her spine. Everyone always wanting something from her. The sun set, bigger and bigger as it got closer to the earth. Photographs of Mads and Peder stared at her from the walls, the water would freeze to ice on the lakes and the icicles would hang down to her eyes, there was no way out, frost mist in an ice-cold house, sick children with fevers, the story would repeat itself, and there was no rightful heir on the farm. Everything flickered so silently. Pressure pushing in from without and out from within. Everything was going somewhere at full speed, her stomach so soft under her dress and her pillow so close to her navel, her thoughts tracking backwards in the middle of her head, a simple good deed. This was the love she had practiced and rehearsed. Pragmatic. Economic. Learned. Belle lay on her side with silent breaths and icy fingers, way down under the woolen blankets, with rag socks and a hot-water bottle. Her pelvis cracked as she lay there, in sweat and haze, the future was rubbing right against her pelvic bone, and then it just happened, so pure and innocent, nine months later her belly was flat and Belle came out onto the porch with a little boy in her arms.

The quiet house, the dark windows. Mother and son. Belle held her child so close that no one could see his face, the little heir, so close to her chest, under her linen shirt. Right on her skin. She rocked him back and forth, she kissed his little head, heard the little hopeful sounds, the angels singing, her breasts bursting. The only rightful heir. Mother and child rocked in the wind, each with a swollen heart. The purest of the pure. They oozed unpredictability. She lifted Philip up and the sun shone through him. He was a true copy of his father, pale white, staring out into eternity. His veins blue just beneath the skin. Belle rocked and rocked her little child. She saw the sofa cushions, the carpets and flowers, the vast plains landscape, the watercolors out in the fields, everything that bled into each other and played along the ridge, above the barn and the mountains, between the insects and her daughters. Flecks of sunlight settled over her eyes. There was no reason to hold back. The grasshoppers sang and Belle stared at the black butterflies out in the garden, a sharp look, straight in the eye, it was death staring back at her.

A LOT OF
LETTERS

T HE PERSONAL ADS peered up at Belle. Thick newspaper pages covered the whole kitchen table, could it
really be so easy? This silent trust, it seemed so strange, that
someone would want to just give themselves away like that.
And now here they were, begging and pleading for her to
find them. It seemed so one-dimensional, so naked. Some of
them just didn't understand that they shouldn't give away all
their belongings. But that's what they did, they wrote in to
the newspaper and said they were willing to offer everything.
Anytime. They were truly willing to give away everything
they owned, to a strange woman. Belle studied the ads, some
people were just doomed to fail.

The longing had been so naked and sore for so long and
now it stretched like a yawning chasm into her heart. Mads
was dead, Peder was dead, Ray Lamphere was walking
around with his hungry face out in the middle of the fields,
God, I need someone to hold me, Belle whispered out at the yard.

The red watercolor above the sky was so thin at the edges, there was nothing here she could hold on to. The church bells tolled their warning peals, she heard a crunch in her spine as the tip of her pen slid across the paper, *I want you to come here and be mine.*

The sun's rays had warmed the envelopes and she lay them against her cheek. She felt a tickling inside her jaw. She wasn't afraid anymore, she had been able to extract Philip's inheritance and it finally felt like she had some air under her wings. She used the letter opener and the paper tore against the sharp blade. The handwriting, her name, the ink twisted around into the big B. Everything was so personal, it seeped through the paper, it was now or never. The answers had come so painfully slowly, but of course they wanted to meet her, right away if possible, the sooner the better. Belle hid the little stack up in the bedroom and every night, after the children were in bed, she sat at the desk and counted on her fingers, counted her letters and wrote her answers.

But it didn't happen fast enough and everything welled up inside her again. Her sensitive face couldn't stand this lull. The wet little warmth in her belly, she sat there with her heart in her throat and sent her personals in to all the Scandinavian newspapers in the area. She wrote and changed diapers, she did everything she could to make sure it came out right, in the right arrangement, that they understood who she was and that she truly was interested in them. She cooked, made coffee, paid the farm workers. She was an upstanding woman, they could count on that. Belle kept busy, she bought nice new dresses for the girls, she fried the meat in the pan with big pats of butter, cut it up into little pieces for them on their plates, and kept Philip for herself. She sold her sausages at the market and put the money in the bank. The banknotes might be wet from rain and sweat after a long day but she dried them, up in the attic or in front of the fireplace, before collecting them and hiding them in the envelopes on the bookshelf. She hid them as well as she could so that Ray wouldn't be tempted. Humming softly, she rocked Philip to sleep, the infinite motherly softness, entirely wordless, what connected her to anyone? Mother and child, one of the world's simplest movements, the fat ran a little way out of the corner of her mouth and dripped onto the letter paper on the kitchen table. Belle looked at her handwriting, the snaking big B, it really was hers, the same as ever, what would happen had to happen and what had to happen would happen, she licked the envelope and folded down the edge, she held it against her cheek for a long time as if to seal it with everything good. Her eyes sparkled. The grease on her fingers made the envelope transparent and the words showed through the paper, she ended with the same sentence every time, *our love is greater than anyone else can understand.*

No doubt about it—there was great love in these letters. It burned through the paper, the Scandinavians were a people full of longing, so far from home, they came looking for her with such trembling and doubting and Belle answered them all as fast as she could, *we're going to be all alone with each other,* she trembled as she wrote it, *can you imagine anything better?* Warmth filled her head and crept all the way out into her fingertips, Belle needed a Norwegian, someone with money, someone who knew the language and the history of the ice-cold darkness. Northern light squirmed in her arms, she wrote and wrote for dear life. The truth lay right there in front of her, shining and clear. Love was the only thing that could save her.

The whole country was filled with longing and the Scandinavian newspapers raised these men up into the light so everyone would know what they were longing for. The light really was insistent over here, and it really hurt to love, it was like being skinned alive, and yet everyone took every chance they could get, every time. Full-grown adults, it was absolutely insane, Belle turned the photographs of Mads and Peder to the wall, she didn't need more promises now about what love should really look like. How a real woman should behave. Belle used her red tongue and licked the next envelope, food, children, house and home, she felt fearless, she sealed the message and promised with her whole heart, *I truly believe we're going to be together forever.* Belle smiled and looked out at Clear Lake, the treetops moving in slow-motion, the birds flying through the sky in huge circles and the field teeming with butterflies. The world was whole.

If you come visit me, you'll never want to leave. She felt relieved as she wrote it, it really was that simple. She felt the strange weightless sensation that would fill her when it all was said and done. She dipped her pen in the ink and squinted at the paper, she tried her best to curve the letters in the right direction without putting her wrist and elbow down on the paper. All so that the inkwell wouldn't tip over and the sentences be destroyed, word after word, everything went so deep, everyone would get their answer, just as long as it didn't all flow together. It was like being underwater in a completely silent world, filled with God's light. When Peder left her it was like she had fallen, she was without a soul, without language, without Heaven, there was no one who reached out his arms for her and took care of her. And the longest movement of all was neither love nor desire, it was the butterfly wings in the garden, it was death, the eye always trying to make eye contact, the longest eternal flicker. Belle sat until her eyes were red and her shoulders sore. Every candidate would be evaluated, preferably include picture, absolutely must be Norwegian. She wound her braid tighter, fixed it with the hairpin, *my men*. The restless candle moved in time with her pupils. Belle sat there with these tiny movements, *I long to get to know you better*. It rushed through her. Her tongue kept gliding over new envelopes, the trembling, the pleading piece of skin that just wanted to lean against her, her tongue licked the last edge, she felt the light of God inside her, the gentle rocking there were no words for. The truth was as strong as the lie, she no longer knew where one began and the other ended but it felt just as strong every time, the warmth in her chest, the sentences on paper, iliac crest on pelvic joint, *no woman is happier than I am now.*

THERE'S LOVE
IN HELL TOO

B ELLE WAS TOTALLY DRUNK on herself. Her hands shook. *Sell everything you own and come to me.* She really could be that direct, then at least it went a little faster. Because they came, every time. The glorious landscape of the South Dakota sky floated before her, glistening in the dark slime, she could see everything so clearly if she only got a little distance. All her lakes, the wet eyes drilling down into the landscape, the long clever roots, every man should see them. They had to understand how beautiful it all actually was. This was what it was all about: making the earth as beautiful as God had made Heaven, what else could a living man or woman ask for? The reflections filled her up, she let the strange hands pull her hair down, it was the most liberating thing she knew. She just let it happen, and she brought them down to the lake every time, to where the treetops cast their shadows across the oily surface of the water. Belle sank down in the sunlight, sprawled out on the grass. She just wanted them to see her, see how strongly two people can feel each other's closeness, how naked you are before God, how much you have to be willing to take from another person. She almost begged, *just come to me, with everything you have.* And they came and she showed off everything she had, giggling and proud like a little girl who's accomplished something for the first time. *It's absolutely incredible, isn't it?* Belle couldn't stop, they really had to see everything she owned.

Olaf Lindboe had fallen asleep right away, and Belle lay awake with the blood pumping in her chest and the slimy water murmuring in her lungs. His big hand had pushed her down to the ground, down there by the lake, his hand had gone way over the line and had marked both inside and outside and Belle didn't even know if he'd understood what she was trying to show him. There was something about her center of gravity, she felt her own body let go, down there, she had moved weightlessly somewhere between thought and world, but Olaf hadn't realized a thing and he hadn't let go until she stopped moving down there. And Belle had been scared to death, it hadn't been fun anymore. She was just trying to tease him a little, but he was completely different than in his letters and he followed every order without a single critical question. Belle believed in her heart that Olaf had given her just that, the innermost heart of his innermost heart, and had revealed himself right before her eyes. That's what was so brutal, and he hadn't said no even though she'd begged him to, and his hands had been so greedy, and she'd felt the wet grass grow in her mouth. She saw it from a long way away, everything dozing half-awake in this house, everything that wouldn't sleep; her fur coat on the floor down in the hall guarded her like an animal twisted inside out but there was no protection to be found, not anywhere. That's what Belle had begun to understand, and Olaf was no angel. He was insecure and uncomfortable and had only fused with her into a big hungry eye. It flickered before her eyes, he had been so scared when she showed him how hungry she really was, as if he wasn't prepared for the fact that there had to be a balance. Belle remembered his look from the night before, the unsure smile when for a few seconds he didn't realize what was going to happen.

But fortunately it had passed, and the closer to each other they'd stood, the more convinced he became. She had felt him against her body and he'd been so beautiful that she almost had to laugh. She felt the relief all the way down to her bones when he finally kissed her, this was an eternal day when love was born, that's how pure it could still be, she felt it with perfect clarity. Just like the first time. Belle lay there and studied what made up his outside: pores, moles, a network of blood vessels. It was always so much more beautiful than she thought, a person completely defenseless in bed. It was perfectly clear, everything was stripped of meaning, all this worthless love made her so sad, even the urge for death wasn't strong enough to pull her along. Deepest of all, Belle had promised Olaf gigantic, tremendous love, the great inexplicable love they had both wanted so badly for so long, he had come with all his money and everything he owned, and she had given it to him. It was almost too much, the shock in his eyes when he realized he'd almost killed her. She just wanted to feel him where she wasn't supposed to. Life could feel so fragile through someone else's eyes. Belle peered into his face, every feature so pure, so innocent. She knew that another letter was coming soon but she couldn't stop looking at him. *We're soulmates*, Olaf Lindboe had said down by the lake. But it wasn't true, they weren't soulmates, they never had been and never would be, and the last vestige of light rode through him like an echo of loneliness. She put her hand on his cheek one last time, *what we have together, the two of us, no one else needs to know anything about it*, Belle whispered.

There had been something peaceful about the position his body was in. She got up from bed and got dressed, looked at the lifeless body and felt indifference in every movement. Death had obviously taken hold of him, that sharply cut body was not worth a thing. Belle whispered very softly, he had no way to hear it, *it's dreadful to fall into the hands of the living God*. The glass of water on the dresser reflected the golden glow, as if the water was mirroring the morning sun melting over the ridge. Was this a foretaste of eternity? It had been so easy, his corpse-pale face, his infinitely warm hand. It had happened so fast.

The smell of the barn burned in her nose, the unpleasant stench of burnt blood and manure crept in everywhere, the thin brown slime murmured as the saw blade laboriously sliced its teeth across the thigh bone. She shoveled the cold ashes into the bucket while thoughts floated through her like thin Bible paper. She thought of the hearse that had come to fetch Peder that time, how cold and gray everything had been. A muscle twitch passed through her and settled behind her eyes, she felt the warmth in her chest. *Love will come and conquer all*, she whispered, almost threatening. But there was no one there to hear her. Belle had never been able to lie, but she had never found it easier to tell the truth, Belle knew God's will was strong but it was also merciless, it was gruesome and hard. She felt the abyss inside her, this was a love story that gaped open at too much, it was just going to go on and on until at last it healed itself.

Birds chirped and flies dozed in the thin curtains, hope lay in infected yellow drops in the corner of her eyes, the kneeling soft act was behind her, it was totally obvious, God's will was God's will, Belle tried to gently hum a little something to herself, *we'll meet here by the river*, but her voice couldn't sustain itself. Belle cleared her throat and stopped, she dipped the sugar cube into the coffee cup and met the eyes of the girls on the other side of the breakfast table, she

173

sucked down the sugar as they devoured their pancakes. The bittersweet taste spread through her. Belle took a sip of the coffee, the girls asked where Olaf had gone, *he didn't want to live like us, the way we live.* They looked at her, eyes wide, little mouths glistening with butter and sugar, *the way we have to live.* She looked sternly at all three girls. The shimmering film of grease from the pan coated the kitchen cupboards, the burnt taste of pancakes clung to her palate, the open windows filled the kitchen with summer air, the angel in her bed was gone. The smell of fried butter and fresh-brewed coffee mingled with the smell of fresh manure, another new day was getting started. Olaf had met his fate with eyes open. Belle had kept nothing back, she had held his gaze the whole time and in that moment everything had existed at once and his dead eyes had stared up at her when she dropped his head into the gunny sack. She thought about what he had said that night, *I love you,* he'd said, but Belle couldn't accept it, she had seen his disappointment and uncertain grin when she sat next to him and stroked his forehead, *no one who loves with their whole self can survive it.*

The water lilies shone out on the water like little lanterns. She put her swollen lips to the envelope, gently, sat there with a strangely absent smile. The impossibility of hope. Forgiveness in its utopian circulation. Her lipstick had smeared, color along the edge like a thin pink border. Everything had rubbed off. The corners of her mouth were about to burst, her men in there and around the whole desk, her beautiful mouth along the edge. A beautiful, battered affair. A new mouth and gaping, screaming body, she was on her way back into the story. Belle looked at her hands, they chose the truth and the lie in one and the same quick turn, cracked skin stretched over her knuckles. Belle held the little cross up to her mouth and kissed it. Everyone was so desperate, they whipped their horse until it was exhausted and then turned up on her stoop out of breath with money everywhere, as if they'd just stuffed it into their jacket linings without even thinking that someone might rob them on the way, but they did as she said, every single time. And each time Ray put the big wet animal in the stable.

I long for you more and more every day, her words almost didn't feel real. It was so strong. The letters of each word shone from the paper. Belle knew that she couldn't decide who would love her and how, *just come to me, I'll be nice.* She felt the candle singe her neck, God's burning gaze, she saw everything beyond it in the darkness, in glimpses, the flowing sweat of love, the lit memorial candles. A puff of air fluttered the newspaper, open with her latest ad in the middle of the page: Wanted – Woman, owner of a well situated and valuable farm in first class condition, seeks a good and reliable man as her partner. A small sum of cash is required; a first class security will be provided. Inquire: C.H., Scandinavian Office.

Belle sat hunched over her desk, the night smelled soggy and old, she slid the letter opener along the edge and cut the envelope open in a graceful little movement, she heard her own voice from way in back, *I'll be nice, I promise.*

THE ABSENCE OF
A LOVE STORY
IS ALSO A
LOVE STORY

B ELLE'S LIFE was a thin film of coincidences. A new
man always knocked on the door, peaceful, determined,
almost suffocatingly accurate every time. Belle leaned forward, every time, *I'm Belle*. Everything was burnt off at the
edges, her round soft voice sheared away. She tried to swallow
but her throat was all stretched out, completely vulnerable,
she reached out toward him and invited him in as quick
as she could before her voice broke. *I'm Kristen*, he finally
said when his hand reached hers. Her whole upper body
sagged slightly when he said his name, a silent little crack,
what was going to happen now? The relief was knife-sharp
when she got yet another try. A star plunged across the sky,
she turned her head to follow it, her eyes sparkled as if the
remains of the star were plunging into her. Softly, softly, she
studied him, she let her gaze slip over his tanned skin like a
feather, *Welcome, Kristen, would you like to hang your coat over there?*
Belle was just as hopeful every time, she really tried to be as

honest and straightforward as she could possibly be, but how should she tell the story? Would he accept it? She took his suitcase and pointed into the living room, where the curtains were drawn and the furniture waited in darkness. The room had baked in the sun all morning and oozed stuffiness. He took a couple of steps into the room, the flies were butting against the windowpane, the whole summer was buzzing in there. He hesitated for a few seconds before taking a bottle out of his travel bag. Her red blood circulated through her white body and Belle's hand shook as she poured the wine into the glasses. The wine sloshed and left dark rings on the dining table. Belle heard the birds start to unleash their tormented cries up above the treetops, *our love is greater than anyone else can understand*, Belle gave a start and looked at him, Kristen was repeating word for word what she'd written to him, and she nodded in recognition. The moonlight made his whole face so pale, there was something about the veil over his eyes, the distance between his legs planted so firmly in the middle of the floor, as if it was a deliberate act, he wanted to know everything, *I've never met anyone like you*, Kristen Hindklev went on, excited, and he raised his glass in a toast. She tried her best and raised her glass to her mouth and looked at him over the rim with her big ice-blue eyes, *I think you'll be glad you did*, she said softly and clinked the glasses. She took a big gulp and swallowed. Kristen looked at her, put a finger under her chin and lifted her head so that she had to meet his gaze. Belle moistened her lips, *it's strange, isn't it?* She made a cautious go of it, *I've had stranger things happen to me*, he replied, looking at Belle as if he could make her do things she didn't want to do. Belle tried to laugh but the soft lingering laugh got stuck in her throat. She swallowed the rest of the glass in one gulp and took a few light little steps up the stairs before turning around and holding her arm out to him. Merging together with another person was like drowning, it was just a matter of staying afloat for long enough at a time, Kristen started to open her corset as soon as they were past the bedroom door, her stomach loosened, at last she could catch her breath.

Kristen Hindklev took her into his arms in the bedroom, he held her, he took a few steps from side to side. They danced quietly, cheek to cheek, soundlessly, barefoot on the floor. They hovered in almost complete silence there in the early morning; alcohol shone in their eyes. It was so quiet in those minutes separating night and day, she felt his heart through his clothes, his pulse of survival, his dizziness and the big gasp through her belly. She was horrified by what he brought out in her. He had wrapped his hand around hers and held it to his heart. He hummed softly in her ear and was so light on his toes, the most beautiful man in the world. She couldn't stop loving him. The sun spread out warmly over the rest of the world, getting stuck between streets and rooftops. When morning came they fell asleep on the bed, exhausted, while the day slipped soundlessly by outside the window. Everything seemed so far away. She promised herself that she would do everything to keep this. To hold him tight and be careful. Not scare him, just cuddle. The world out there seemed so infinitely far away, everything was so detached from ordinary life. She was ready to relearn the power of love, she felt the vibrations in the ground and she heard it whisper every morning, it rolled through the room like thunder, the flash of two lovers sleeping tight, right up next to each other. She felt it inside her, this must be what eternity looked like.

Fear sat clenched like a cold claw in Belle's spine, she had a strong feeling of being at an endpoint, at a cliff she was about to slip off of. She no longer had a perspective on the world, it didn't need her and with its jerky shattered light it reminded her of that fact as often as it could. She could see it in him, the moment just before dying, in the silence before the death rattle when sometimes you were permitted to see something completely new. There was never any protection, not now, not later. The skin had torn and the guts lay twisted inside out, Kristen Hindklev lay there on the ground like the little child he was, all alone, like an open wound exposed in the world. She took out a knife. A butcher knife. White clouds gathered together over her head. It must have been a hunting knife, it lay soft and firm in her hand like a mirror reflecting the whole sky in the blade, and the sky saw exactly what was happening. The sun stretched its long radiant arms down to the ground, blinded and destroyed. She looked down at Kristen. It was too late. She stood glued to the ground, the blood smelled like iron, the body was steaming. The sky was reflected in the bloody knife blade. The yellow light coated her face with a last bruise. His dark red lips, something opened there then, something totally alien, Kristen saw all this for the first time lying there before Belle. She saw it in his eyes, just then, same as before, what was inside a person raised up into the light and laid bare. And when light was welcomed in the pain was gone, the open face, the dripping newborn before her. He had closed his eyes and sunk into the shining moment. Belle had really believed him when he said he wanted to stay with her. Her lips moved, almost without moving, *I only gave you what I thought you wanted*, and now he lay there with black lips and open eyes. Belle stared at the broken body, blood ran down into the earth. She pushed the arms and legs and torso into the hole and shoveled the soil over it. She looked at the grave, the shovel couldn't quite cover up what it had done. The crying had left her, the silver lake had gathered up all her tears, it lay there mirror-bright, ice-cold. She saw nothing new, he had nothing worth seeing. He was a fallen man, buried against his will, he hadn't known what was waiting for him. Her carnivorous heart was exactly that simple, moments of closeness, a big black wound. A whole European map of dead men.

Belle stood by the bedroom window and felt the wind bring in the smell of dirt from the freshly plowed property. She'd had to start digging deeper so that the girls wouldn't notice all the little mounds in the dirt, her wrists hurt. The light radiating from a foreign eye, that's what she wanted to drown in. In someone else's ground zero, someone else's story. That was what she had done. Her men spread out across the sky like warning flares, dripping red holes between finger marks and bruises and endless yearning bodies, she saw how it left such a clear blue mark in the skin the next day, where Ole Budsberg had tensed up and tried to defend himself. It was perfectly clear how deep he had gone, how blue it could get. Belle traced the circumference of the mark on her thigh with her finger. It wasn't that bad, but it wasn't good either. The blue hours, the dull blue light, his resistance in her body, she never knew if it was a curse or a blessing that there were always more men out there. She went to get a shawl and draped it over her shoulders, *love can't forgive anything*, the candlelight flickered, there was another storm coming. She turned and looked at the dead body on the floor, pale and cold. An ice-cold foretaste. There was always more to say, but she had ruined everything already.

Belle had laid him down right next to her before the blood slowly trickled out of his body, *baby, baby, baby*. Belle had raised her arm quite silently, she lit a cigarette with the glow from the previous one. She had played God. The bluish smoke curled in the sunshine. Her hands were so rough and foul against her soft lips. Everything was just variations of hard and heavy, light and soft, skin and bone, there weren't a hundred seamless transitions, she felt it literally, her heart couldn't stand anymore, the oozing burn, nothing turned beautiful all by itself, *what connects one person to another?* But everything was just repetitions of the same awful dreams, the hand of God waking her up in the middle of the night and carrying her over to the cliff. Her thighs rubbed against each other and the white skin flared up and suddenly a new man was standing there, all by himself. Imagine being found in a hole in the ground, Belle looked at him, he didn't understand anything, when he'd realized he was allowed to come he got right on his horse and he was so out of breath when he rode up to her door, his back all sweaty. Totally desperate. Belle opened her lips a little more, hope lay in the corners of her mouth, dry, overheated, with congealed spit, her cigarette glowing in the darkness. The whole time John Moe was unloading his things from the cart she kept hearing the echo of her own voice, it lay in her mouth in the most unpleasant way, *now you're here with me. And you'll never want to leave.*

The face always opened wide, opened all the way up. And then came the blood, dark and gushing as if it would never stop. A ribbon of fat along the skin, head over arm, torso over thigh bone, shining open cracks all the way in. It flowed so clearly and there was so much, like God did it on purpose. She felt the gentle breeze make everything rock and sway, the light winked between the yellow ears of corn and stabbed her in the chest, *from dust you are and to dust you shall return*, a cold pool of dead bodies and pure fear. It ran ice-cold, all the way into her arms, and the thin light fell so far down, between the stalks, all the way down to the bottoms of the lakes, the slow perdition, the pale light of salvation. The long arms of God. She carried their lives in her arms, like newborn babies. The heart lay there, thin as a butterfly's wing, cut out of the chest. There was something pure about it too—how the knife cut all the way down to the bone, through cartilage, into marrow. She could take the head off the body with her bare hands. It was something completely separate, their lives just hung by a thread, it was totally arbitrary, and that's what they were so afraid of, so afraid that they begged her: *I don't want to die alone.* But death came with neither mercy nor forgiveness, it all happened in the sun, in broad daylight. Belle looked at her lovers lying there with widened eyes, she gave them the tenderest look she had. She gave the knife one last turn to make sure that all the life had left his body, *no one is easy to love.*

Belle put the arms right next to the body, as if he was hugging himself. She thought about what Nellie had said, about how you couldn't live in your own arms, but you could, you could live in God's arms, in God's name. And right in front of her lay a body, alone in its own embrace. That was just how she had lived, that was what she'd been surrounded by, that was the only thing she wanted—to get them all under her skin until the skin couldn't be stretched any farther, until she opened, and leaked, until you could see her heart in the open gap, until her blood trickled out, until she could feel the whole world on her tongue, her cheek against the light, the biggest streak of them all, *this is what I have, this is what I am.* She got blood on her skirt and hands and started to shake violently. This was where it all started, this was where everything came into focus. This was the sad connection with something human. The blood ran silently down to her fingertips and vanished into the fresh soil, *to the pure all is pure.* Belle wiped her hands on her skirt. Everyone wanted grief to be so beautiful but there was nothing beautiful about any of this.

It took a while before Belle noticed that the girls were standing in the kitchen doorway, looking at her, *you must have a big heart,* they said, their voices soft with sleep. Belle put her hand on her chest, *since there's room for so many people.* She felt the traces of hardened sperm on her forehead, up by her hairline, it flaked off like sunburned skin, Belle didn't know what she was supposed to feel, she looked at her girls, so small, hair tangled from sleep, *there are some kinds of love you can't explain,* she said. They just stared at her, not making a

187

sound, she saw their white fists, their small tight hands, the red light had started to press against the window and the candles flickered on the table, *sometimes you just get something you didn't know you wanted, a bit like how I got you.* The whites of their eyes were completely blank. Her love had grown too big, it had forced its way into them, red shadows curved in their faces, it went so deep. They thought they could make themselves invisible over there in the corner, but she saw them with perfect clarity. The sky came in through the window, across the floor and the rugs, over her eyes, like blood pouring in from outside. The whites of their eyes trembled there in the darkness, she felt the vibrations through the floorboards, the longings she had spread with the wind, the big greedy mouth that only wanted more and more, *everyone deserves another chance.*

The rain made the earth so wet and slippery, reality turned slowly unrecognizable, and their faces were ground down, no one would remember who they even looked like, they would see just the remains of a stranger's jaw and some gold teeth glittering in the mud. The meat grinder sat next to the stack of letters in the bedroom, an almost vulgar coincidence to remind her of Peder's failings, her own limits. Night dozed in the open window, the children huddled together in the middle of her bed, the thin cream-white nightgowns, fabric curling at the slightest touch. She stroked their foreheads and felt their warmth, the sweet scent of freshly blooming lilacs and curdled milk. It was as if their weight clung to hers and dragged her down to the floor, the stars twinkling like shimmering little eyelids. *Lord, let your light shine upon us.* She looked at her beautiful children, they were too pure for this world.

Outside the window the ground buckled, the grass had grown almost imperceptibly in the yard and covered the small pits but the fresh graves hadn't had time to settle. Carrion flies gathered above the mounds, revealing every fallen man. She'd held lye over Andrew Helgelien's face until it disappeared, he lay there so helpless, she could feel it, he lay there and watched her, two marbles in the middle of his face, hard and ice-cold. Belle found herself at the end of the world. She saw it with perfect clarity, the bright sharp edges running down into infinity. She had sunk the bodies into the mud, they lay there covered with trash and heavy stones which kept pushing them farther and farther away from the earth's surface. The morning light came in, between the barn and the stable, it spread and was reflected in the dewdrops on the grass. The smell of iron filled her nostrils, it was sickening, finally it was over, it went through her like the glow from a cigarette, just as suddenly, just as gone. She saw the last soft mouth taut and tense between the tufts of grass, a gaping hole straight down into the ground, slowly it filled with dirt, the eyes disappeared, it was like his whole self was radiating upwards in his two arms.

Her gaze swept across the graves with the same dispassionate intensity as death itself. Everything she didn't have to deal with anymore. She had gotten what she needed. She didn't need more money, or more closeness, there was nothing more that could be taken from her. The first bodies had started to decay and the treetops were drowning in the light of the bleeding spring sun. The smell of sulfur, manure, and old water covered the farm. Unzipping men's flies, the light shifting behind the eyelids, all that was over now. She rocked Philip on her shoulder, shifting her weight from one foot to the other. It was totally quiet this early in the morning. The lake was singing and the freshly slaughtered pigs were steaming out in the yard, it could have been a coincidence but it wasn't. She put the bucket of rat poison next to the kerosene tank. Her face was swollen and her eyes sat on her face like black lilies.

The rut was so intense in the stable. She heard the animals knocking around in their stalls, pacing and pacing, they wouldn't stop circling. The dim light entered through the cracks in the wall and she couldn't tell the shadows apart from the bodies but the sounds were perfectly clear. She ran her hand along the wall, the present slipped by beneath her fingertips, the end stuck in her windpipe, no one could know when it all just ended. When no more air reached the lungs. When someone was never going to come back and get you. The stallions whinnied loudly and slammed into the walls, who sets out on a long trip with an uncastrated young horse? Belle took a handful of hay and went over to one of them. Foam frothed at the corners of its mouth and its ears were pulled back. Swaying head, soft muzzle, it was the horse that had come with Andrew, the difficult young horse, completely unusable. Her stable was full of riderless animals abandoned in the thunderstorm. She opened the gate and walked into the stall, and their body heat oozed like frost around them. The big brown face. She took one of the brushes that was in the bucket and started to groom his warm body. Belle leaned her cheek in and closed her eyes. She felt the lines of the whipstrokes, the final blow of the arm that always drove them farther in. Large pupils fluttered stiffly, horseshoes scraped against the floor, an enormous feeling of being overpowered, she was in contact with something bigger, and suddenly he just stood completely still, steaming with body heat. Belle felt the fear tighten in her chest, she opened the gate as carefully as she could and closed it without a sound. She turned around one last time. Time had settled into them and the acrid smell of wet hay, blood, and urine forced its way in everywhere. The wind blew across the rooftops, howling into the cracks as if hauling a bottomless pain with it. These beautiful worthless creatures, they'd had no way of knowing what they were getting into.

When evening came, Belle walked around the house and closed one window after the other. She met her own gaze in the glass and saw what the children had been afraid of. Her reflection shone silently back at her, she saw everything: its unpredictability, its blank expressionlessness. The simplicity of the monumental. Everything that could kill someone.

QUIET HOUSE. Dark windows. There was something about all the flowers Belle had kept in the dining room, as if it was decorated for mourning and burial at all times, the overwhelming smell had always made it so hard to breathe. It was always so suffocating in the house, that's what people who'd been there always said. Both Nellie and her family. In the ruins they found the remains of a letter in Belle's handwriting, the only visible words being: "It seems that I've changed since then. For the past few weeks, despair and anxiety have weighed upon me. I don't know why."

On April 28th, 1908, at 4:00 a.m., the Gunness farm burned to the ground. The dogs usually barked whenever anyone approached, but they were tied behind the house that night and they hadn't made a sound. The firefighters couldn't put out the fire and had to wait until the flames died down. The only thing left, after the fire, were the cellar ruins. When they started digging on the property, they found the bodies of ten dismembered men buried in different parts of the yard. In the cellar ruins they found the remains of three charred little children and a headless woman. The first two they found, the girls, were lying face down. The boy was found under one of the girls. He was lying on the woman's left arm. When they finally dug up the whole property, it turned out that the remains corresponded to the bodies of a total of thirty men, and that the eldest girl, Jennie, was buried in the yard. Ray Lamphere was arrested and convicted of arson. Belle Gunness had disappeared without a trace. She was never seen again.

Lovingly Acknowledged

Sigrid Lien – *Pictures of Longing* / Sylvia Elizabeth Shepherd – *The Mistress of Murder Hill: The Serial Killings of Belle Gunness* / Hans Melien – *Belle Gunness: Serial Killer from Selbu* / Bodil Stenseth – *Mrs. Muus's Lawsuit* / Truman Capote – *In Cold Blood: A True Account of a Multiple Murder and Its Consequences* / Vigdis Hjorth – *If Only*; *Third Person Singular* / Aina Basso – *The Child* / Clarice Lispector – *Near to the Wild Heart*; *The Hour of the Star* / Naja Marie Aidt – *When Death Takes Something from You Give It Back* / Yahya Hassan – *Yahya Hassan: Poems*; *Yahya Hassan 2* / Sara Stridsberg – *The Gravity of Love*; *Darling River*; *The Antarctica of Love* / Per Olov Enquist – *Downfall*; *The Parable Book* / Marilynne Robinson – *Gilead* / Molly Nilsson – *American Express* / Janet Jackson – *janet.* / Lana Del Rey – *Born to Die* / Gunvor Hofmo – "There Is No More Everyday" / Ida Linde – *The Murderer's Mom* / Sara Lundberg – *The Bird in Me Flies* / Lena Lindgren – *Morgenbladet* newspaper / *Only Belle: A Serial Killer from Selbu* (documentary) / *Regarding Susan Sontag* (documentary) / *Joan Didion: The Center Will Not Hold* (documentary) / Janet L. Langlois – *Belle Gunness: The Lady Bluebeard* / Lillian de la Torre – *The Truth about Belle Gunness* / Emilie Nicolas – "Who's Gonna Love You?"

ABOUT THE AUTHOR

Victoria Kielland's first book, the 2013 short prose collection *I Lyngen* (*In the Heather*), was shortlisted for the Tarjei Vesaas debutant prize. In 2016, Kielland's first novel, *Dammyr* (*Marsh Pond*), was shortlisted for the Youth Critics' Prize, and the literary committee of the Norwegian Authors' Union awarded her the Norwegian Booksellers' primary writer's scholarship. *My Men* is her breakthrough novel, published to rave reviews in Norway in 2021 and now set to be published in fourteen languages. *My Men* was awarded the Thorleif Dahl Prize and the Swedish Academy's Dobloug Prize.

ABOUT THE TRANSLATOR

Damion Searls has translated more than fifty books of clas-
sic modern literature, most recently Thomas Mann's *New
Selected Stories*, Jon Fosse's *Septology*, and *Bambi*. His own writing
includes fiction, poetry, criticism, *The Inkblots*—a history of
the Rorschach Test and biography of its creator, Hermann
Rorschach—and *The Philosophy of Translation*, forthcoming.